She stepped into the darkened auditorium. "Anybody here?" she called. No one answered. The door to a small room about the size of a walk-in closet was open, and the light was on inside.

In the room she saw that the cabinet was padlocked. Hearing someone in the doorway behind her, she jumped.

"What are *you* doing here?" Grant asked.

The door slammed shut and Cindy heard someone snap a lock in place. She heard scuffling feet and knew before she even tried the door that they were locked in.

Grant turned quickly and pushed against the door. He tried forcing it open but soon saw that it was no use. "This is real cute. Did you arrange it?"

"Me? Why would I do something this stupid?"

"Well, obviously the door didn't just close by itself."

Cindy pushed past him and began banging on the door and yelling, "Mollie Lewis, you come back here and unlock this door!"

FAWCETT GIRLS ONLY BOOKS

SISTERS

THREE'S A CROWD #1

TOO LATE FOR LOVE #2

THE KISS #3

SECRETS AT SEVENTEEN #4

ALWAYS A PAIR #5

SISTERS

ALWAYS A PAIR

Jennifer Cole

FAWCETT GIRLS ONLY • NEW YORK

RLI: VL: Grades 5 + up / IL: Grades 6 + up

A Fawcett Girls Only Book
Published by Ballantine Books
 Published in the United States by Ballantine Books, a division of Random House, Inc., New York, and simultaneously in Canada by Random House of Canada Limited, Toronto.

Library of Congress Catalog Card Number: 86-90894

ISBN 0-449-13012-6

Manufactured in the United States of America

First Edition: August 1986

Chapter One

Balancing a plate of crackers and cheese in one hand and a glass of soda in the other, Cindy carefully made her way into the den. Suddenly she stumbled over something and nearly fell, causing the plate and the crackers to slide to the floor.

"Ow! Why don't you watch where you're going?" her younger sister, Mollie, shrieked, tossing her long blond wavy hair over her shoulder. Cindy frowned as she looked down at Mollie spread out across the middle of the family room, painting her toenails. One foot stuck out comically in front of her with wads of tissue between each toe, and the other one was pulled up tightly next to her as she carefully tried to repair the damage Cindy had done when she bumped into her.

"Can't you find someplace else to do that?" Cindy demanded, setting down her glass on the table and bending down to pick up the spilled crackers.

"I'm watching MTV," Mollie explained as she carefully replaced the top on the bottle of nail polish and surveyed her toes.

Rolling her eyes, Cindy plopped herself down on the couch and picked up the newspaper, opening it to the sports section. She hid behind the paper and munched on crackers while Mollie applied a second coat to her toenails.

Putting the paper down, Cindy sniffed the air. "That stuff really stinks, and I'm trying to eat. Would you please do that in the bathroom?" Smokey, one of the Lewises' cats, jumped onto her lap. She picked him up and stroked his head.

"I'm almost done. Besides, I was here first." Mollie started to whine but stopped. She was watching the TV. "Oh, my gosh, Cindy, look! There he is. Isn't he just the most beautiful hunk you've ever seen?"

"Not really," Cindy said unaffectedly as she glanced up briefly at the TV screen. Mollie could drool over all the long-haired rock stars she wanted, but Cindy preferred reality. Tossing her paper plate into the garbage, she got up. "Be sure you clean all that junk up before Mom gets home," she said.

"Leave me alone. You're as bad as Nicole."

Cindy stepped carefully over the polish and

clippers on the floor and looked down at her younger sister, who was wearing a purple sweatsuit with matching hair ribbon. "I really don't even know why you bother with all that. No one can see your toes anyway."

"So what?" Mollie said with an air of I-know-more-than-you-think-I-do. "Just because you want to look like a slob doesn't mean I have to copy you. I happen to have some pride in myself. If I were you—"

"Actually, I did try painting my toenails once," Cindy interrupted her. "It was in the eighth grade. These three toes here on my left foot got stuck together, and I had a webbed foot for two days."

Knowing it was hopeless, Mollie shrugged her shoulders and went back to painting her toenails.

Carrying Smokey, Cindy climbed the stairs to her room and closed the door behind her, but not before Cinders, their other cat, darted in the door. She gazed at the line of trophies that adorned her room. They were for softball and swimming and surfing and soccer, but not one of them had been for charm or beauty. Those were the kind of trophies her sisters, Mollie and Nicole, would win. Not that Cindy cared; she'd rather be a jock than a beauty queen.

Appraising herself in the mirror, she realized that no one would mistake her for a cover girl, but she didn't think she was a slob. Okay, she didn't wear makeup, but her short blond hair was thick and shiny despite all of her swimming, and her practically year-round tan emphasized her blue eyes. Of course, Mollie would say that mascara or eyeliner would emphasize them better. The phone rang, interrupting her thoughts, and she jumped, running out into the hallway to pick it up.

"Hello."

"Cindy?" It was Anna, one of her best friends. She could hear Mollie asking who it was and covered the receiver to yell, "It's for me." Then she said, "Hi, what's up?"

"Well, a bunch of us thought we'd go three-wheeling this afternoon. We thought maybe you and Grant would like to come along."

"That sounds like fun. Grant's supposed to call me in a little while when he gets finished with some chores. I'll ask him then. What time are you leaving?"

"We'll probably take off at about one. We thought we'd pack some stuff and have a barbecue somewhere."

"Sounds great. Who's going?"

"Duffy and Carey and Mike and just about anyone else who wants to."

"Tell you what; I'll call Grant right now and then I'll call you back just as soon as I know what's up."

Cindy hung up and dialed Grant's number. It rang several times before she finally hung up. Returning to her room, she looked at the clock radio above her bed. It was 10:15. He ought to be calling her soon, so she could wait. In the meantime, she could start scrounging around in the kitchen for things they could take with them.

Cindy was really excited. It had been weeks since she and Grant had done anything with her crowd. She missed her friends, who were all pairing off into couples, too, but still hung around together. They were all good friends and had been together since junior high or grade school. Sometimes it was hard for Grant, who had just transferred to Vista High from Hawaii this year, to understand that she could kid around with Duffy and the other guys, confide in them, and even give them a friendly hug now and then without its meaning anything.

"If I get any calls, I'll be taking a bubble bath," Mollie, appearing in the doorway, informed Cindy.

"You have plans or something? How come you're getting yourself all fixed up?"

"I want to be ready in case anything *does* come up." She had put her hair up in pin curls. Cindy watched her bounce off to the bathroom. Sometimes she wondered why Mollie was in such a hurry to grow up. Actually she wished she could trade places with her now and then so Mollie could be the one who was nearly sixteen and she could be fourteen again.

When she was fourteen, things had been a lot easier. She'd been happy to play volleyball on the beach or softball in the park. The only thing boys were good for at that time in her life was fielding a team or splitting the price of a pizza.

Things sure had changed since Grant came into her life. Now she worried about things she'd never even thought about before. If she did play volleyball on the beach, she worried that she didn't use enough deodorant. When they ate pizza after a game, she worried that the onions might give her bad breath. And now candy bars weren't something you ate during the movie; they were things you passed up because they gave you zits. Yeah, she reflected, life was sure a lot simpler at fourteen.

While she was surveying the contents of the refrigerator, the phone rang. She reached out and picked it up. "You must have been camping out next to the phone," Grant teased her. "That didn't take you long."

"Oh, I was just packing up a few things here in the kitchen, and I was standing right next to it."

"Packing up things? For what?"

"Well, I tried calling you earlier. Anna called. She invited us to go three-wheeling this afternoon with her and Duffy and a bunch of the kids. Doesn't it sound like fun?"

"This afternoon?" he said hesitantly. "Actually, I've already committed us to go bowling with Brian and Julie."

"Oh," she said, trying to keep the disappointment out of her voice.

"But I suppose if you don't want to, I could call and tell them . . ."

"No, it's okay. I like bowling," she said. And she

really did. It was just that she hadn't been with *her* friends in such a long time.

And she had already pictured herself sitting around a roaring fire with Grant's arm holding her close as the hot dogs roasted in front of them. She sighed and forced the idea out of her mind. It wasn't as if there would never be another chance to do those things. The weather was almost perfect around Santa Barbara, and there were lots of Saturdays.

"Look, I'm sorry if you're upset. I just wish you'd have asked me before you made plans for us."

"Did you ask me?" she retorted before she could stop herself.

"What's that supposed to mean? You knew I was going to call you this morning and tell you what we were going to do. Now you're getting all bent out of shape because it's not what you want to do," he said defensively.

He was right. She remembered Grant asking her what she wanted to do, and she'd said, "I don't care. Call me tomorrow when you decide." She listened to the silence on the line. "You're right," she said. "What time do you want to go?"

"I thought I'd pick you up about three and we'd meet Brian and Julie at the bowling alley. Afterward, we can go to Pete's for pizza and maybe see a movie."

He was trying to make it up to her, and Cindy felt like a creep for being angry with him in the first place. She forced herself to sound excited. "Great. I haven't been bowling in ages."

"Good. I'll see you about three." She started to hang up and heard him ask shyly, "You're not still mad, are you?"

"Of course not. It's okay. See you later," she said, and hung up the phone. For the second time that morning, she thought about how much easier it had been to be fourteen and the only one you had to please was yourself.

Pushing the disappointment to the back of her mind, she firmly dialed Anna's number. She hated to tell Anna she wouldn't be able to join them . . . again. She was afraid if this kept up that one day they would stop inviting her along.

Chapter Two

Cindy was putting away the last of the food she'd packed for the picnic they wouldn't be taking when Nicole and her mother walked in, buried beneath sacks of groceries. It never ceased to amaze Cindy that Nicole actually enjoyed going to the grocery store.

The only time Cindy remembered enjoying a trip to the store was one afternoon when she was about six and she and some little boy had raced through the store pretending to be Mario Andretti. It was lots of fun until they crashed into a display of popcorn and the jars had come crashing down around them, spilling little kernels all over the place.

She hadn't even been able to make a quick getaway, because the cart had gotten stuck on the popcorn and it was hard to run because the slippery stuff was everywhere. Her mother had come running over, and she was sent to the car with the stern promise that that would be the last trip she ever made to the grocery store. What her mother had never realized was that the punishment was actually a reward.

She watched them unpack the bags as though they were the bounty from some great treasure hunt. Nicole was talking excitedly about a new recipe she wanted to try. She could understand her mother's interest. After all, she owned her own catering business, Moveable Feasts, but she thought her older sister was plain crazy. Cindy had long ago decided that when she got married, she'd give her husband TV dinners and gift certificates to McDonald's. If he wanted gourmet cooking, she'd buy him a cookbook.

"Are you and Grant going out this evening?" her mother asked from behind the refrigerator door.

"Yeah," she said, sensing it was time to get out of the kitchen.

"Where are you going?" Nicole asked with polite interest.

"Bowling."

"That sounds nice," her mom said, popping up over the top of the door and reaching her hand toward the package of meat on the counter that Nicole handed to her.

"Yeah, well, I'd better go get ready," she said, making a quick exit.

By three o'clock she had convinced herself that she was going to have fun. It had clouded over and almost looked like rain, so maybe it was a good thing they weren't going three-wheeling after all.

When Grant came to pick her up, he looked especially handsome in a powder-blue sweater that set off his blue eyes. Cindy tossed a yellow sweatshirt over her shoulders and looped the sleeves together to hold it on.

They got in Grant's car, a red Trans Am, and the stereo sprang to life when he started the ignition. The music filled the silence as they rode to the bowling alley. She slid over next to Grant to reassure him that everything was fine with her and told herself that she was going to have fun.

Brian and Julie were late, as usual. Julie apologized, making it a point to say that it was all her fault. She took forever to get ready. Cindy critically compared her own faded jeans and tennis shoes with Julie's wool shorts and matching argyle socks and sweater. She was perfectly coordinated, down to the ribbon around her shiny dark hair.

Grant smiled. "We just got here ourselves."

Cindy looked at him. Sure, they'd just arrived—thirty minutes ago.

After Julie tried out several balls and exchanged her shoes for a smaller size, they were finally ready to start bowling. Julie started by dropping her ball and rolling it feebly down the gutter. She turned to Brian and crumbled up in hopeless laughter, so Brian showed her how to hold the ball and concluded that she needed one with smaller holes.

Julie then set her ball on the foul line and rolled it forward, where it lumbered its way toward the gutter and drunkenly dropped in. After they found her a lighter ball, it was finally someone else's turn. During the game Julie managed to put at least one out of every two balls in the gutter. If, by some miracle, she did keep the ball on the alley, it was usually rolling so slowly by the time it reached the end that one pin might stagger and fall. Julie would scream with delight and jump up, clapping her hands. This little display didn't seem to annoy either Brian or Grant, but Cindy could feel her temper rising.

She told herself to stop being so hard on Julie. After all, it wasn't Julie's fault that she would rather have been three-wheeling with people of normal intelligence.

When they finished bowling, Julie had averaged a 62 for the four games, and Cindy had averaged a 194. Julie was still fidgeting with readjusting her socks when Grant came back from returning their shoes. Cindy picked up her ball, and Grant took his and Julie's both. "I'll put this back. Meet us at the cashier."

Julie smiled sweetly and said, "Thanks, Grant, you're a doll."

Fuming, Cindy put her ball in the rack and went

into the rest room. A few seconds later the door opened and Julie appeared. "Isn't this the most fun?" she gushed. "I wish I could bowl like you. But then you make everything look so easy. I bet you're just a natural athlete, aren't you?"

Cindy was tempted to tell her to save her flattery for the boys. It worked better on them, but she reminded herself that Brian was Grant's friend and Julie was Brian's girlfriend and she couldn't go around insulting her. "It's just a matter of hand-eye coordination," she told her, washing her hands.

"Boy, coordination is one thing I don't have much of." Julie laughed. "I trip over the lines painted on the gym floor." She gave herself one final look and touched up her already perfect makeup. "You ready?"

"Go ahead. I'll be out in a minute."

Julie took hold of the doorknob. "I'll see you in a second, then."

Cindy splashed cold water on her face and told herself to keep her temper in check. She dried her face and came out to find them waiting for her for a change.

"Ready?" Brian asked.

"Sure." She and Grant walked side by side, but she was aware that he didn't make any attempt to hold her hand. It was going to be a great evening, she thought.

At the movies Julie claimed she wasn't hungry, then proceeded to eat all of Brian's popcorn.

Cindy spent a lot of time wondering why girls thought they had to be dizzy to get some guy to think they were cute. Cute. Geez, what a word! She might want some guy to think she was a lot of things, but cute wasn't one of them. Smart, funny, athletic, honest, fair. There were lots of reasons she'd want someone to ask her out, and she hoped none of them came down to just being cute.

The movie was a complete disaster. Cindy finally had to get up and leave in order to come back and ask Grant to move over next to Julie so that he could listen to her ramble on about what a total babe Tom Cruise was. Not only did Julie talk nonstop, but then she wanted them to tell her what she missed because she hadn't been paying attention. Cindy lost track of the number of times she said, "I don't get it."

After the movie and pizza, Grant took Brian and Julie back to Brian's car and dropped them off. He and Cindy didn't say a word to each other most of the way to her house. Finally he stopped the car about a half a block from her house. He looked over at her with a funny expression on his face. "What's the matter with you, Cindy? You were about as much fun as a case of the hives today."

"Me? What did I do?"

"To begin with, did you have to bowl like you were on the *Wide World of Sports* and make Julie look like a fool?"

"Hey, don't blame me. She was doing a pretty good job of that all by herself."

"And you sulked through the pizza and acted like the movie was the worst thing you'd ever seen."

"I'm not sure about the movie. I'll have to see it again sometime. Julie was so busy talking my ear off that I missed most of it."

"Julie's not what's bothering you, and you know it. You're mad at me because we didn't do what you wanted today."

"That's not true." It really isn't, she thought.

"Isn't it? Look, Cindy, I like your friends. It's just that sometimes I like doing things with my friends, too."

"That's all we ever do."

"How can you say that? I hardly see them at all. Besides, it's not easy going out with someone who can make you look second-best at most things."

"Well, why don't I make it easier for you? Maybe Julie has some dingy friend who isn't doing anything next week, and the two of them can entertain you with their Goldie Hawn routine. You can probably rearrange her life, and she'll love it, because she'll be too dumb to notice you're running it for her."

Furious, she grabbed the door handle and jumped out of the car. She'd walk home. Cindy heard the door open and Grant call out to her, but she kept walking and wouldn't look back.

She heard his footsteps running to catch up to her, but she wouldn't give him the satisfaction of turning around to look. Finally, he caught up to her and took her firmly by the arm.

"Look, I don't want some bubblehead like Julie. I like you because you're different. But stop trying to make it impossible for me to like you."

She looked up at his handsome face and felt her anger and resolve melt away. The glow from the streetlight caught his dark, wavy hair as he tilted his head toward her. "I'm sorry. I guess I ruined the evening, didn't I?" she said.

Grant responded by putting his arm around her, and they started to walk toward her house. "Maybe you're right about Julie. I mean, she is cute and everything," he said with a grin. "But sometimes you like to talk to them, too."

Cindy laughed. "Well, if you want them to talk, maybe you should go out with Mollie. She sure can talk."

Grant laughed, displaying his dimple. "Well, I wouldn't go that far."

"Or if you like fashion plates, you could go out with Nicole."

"You're the perfect Lewis for me."

He stopped walking and put both his arms around her. "Correction, the perfect girl."

Cindy smiled and returned Grant's kiss. What had she been making such a fuss about? Grant MacPhearson didn't want a bubblehead—he wanted her.

Chapter Three

The Lewises sat at the restaurant and waited for Cindy to return from yet another trip to the buffet table. Nicole shook her head in wonder as Cindy approached with a steaming plate in front of her. "*Mon dieu!* Are you actually going to eat all that?"

"Energy, Nicole." Cindy frowned, plunging her fork into the overflowing plate. She hated it when Nicole spoke French. But Nicole, who loved everything French and spoke the language fluently, couldn't be stopped.

"But what happens when you get older and your metabolism slows down and you are in the habit of eating like a heavyweight prizefighter?"

"I'll get fat," she said with a smile, and continued to eat, ignoring the disdainful looks of her more delicate sister.

"Well," Mollie said softly, "I think I'll take advantage of the dessert table before we leave."

"But you already had dessert." Cindy looked up.

"Yes, I know, but I didn't eat half my omelet, and that must have saved me two hundred calories, and then I won't actually start my diet until tomorrow. So I'd better make the most of today, because after tomorrow, it's nothing but grapefruit and hard-boiled eggs." She swept off dramatically toward the dessert table.

"Mollie can find an excuse for anything," Cindy commented as she pushed away her plate. She was not quite finished, but she was full, and to be honest with herself, she had taken more than she needed. She was always doing that at all-you-can-eat places.

Mollie returned with a chocolate mousse. Drawing the spoon through the mixture, she explained to her bemused family, "Actually, sugar isn't as bad for you as some people would have you think. Like, when you need quick energy, you can eat sugar and notice the results much faster."

"Sometimes at school," she continued, "I know that if I eat a salad and croutons, I may eat as many as four hundred calories. But a Snickers bar has only two hundred seventy calories, so I eat the Snickers and enjoy lunch more." She smiled triumphantly and drew her spoon out of the creamy mousse toward her mouth.

"Mollie, do me a favor." Cindy laughed. "Don't ever teach logic."

"Hey, Cindy," Mr. Lewis called from the family room, "the Lakers game is starting."

"Coming," Cindy called from the kitchen. Gathering the rest of the brownies onto a tray, she went into the den to join him. As she settled down onto the floor, a large black furry body flopped down beside her. "Hey, Winston. Wanna watch, too?" she asked the dog. The Newfoundland merely looked at her, puzzled. Basketball wasn't Cindy's favorite sport, but she realized she had been ignoring her dad quite a bit lately, and she didn't want to hurt his feelings. She still loved sports as much as ever; it was just that now she spent a lot more time with Grant.

Just before halftime, the phone rang. "Cindy, it's for you," Mollie called.

Cindy answered expecting it to be Grant, but she was surprised to hear Duffy on the other end.

"What are you doing?"

"Nothing much. Just watching the Lakers game."

"Well, a bunch of us are going to get up a game of beach volleyball in a little while. You and Grant want to join us?"

"Sure, that sounds like fun," she said, then hesitated, remembering that she had told herself she'd spend this afternoon with her dad. "Let me check and see what my dad has going for the rest of the day, and I'll call you back."

"You don't need to call. Just meet us at the beach if you want to play."

"Okay."

"And be sure to bring Grant."

"Yeah, I will."

Cindy hung up the phone and went back into the den. "Who was that?" her dad asked, looking up from the TV.

"Duffy. A bunch of the kids are playing volleyball and they wanted me to come."

"Sounds like fun."

"But I thought we were going to watch the game," she said, hoping for a way out.

"Actually, it's not a very good game. The Sonics are running away with it. Go ahead and play volleyball. I really have some things I need to work on this afternoon."

"Are you sure?"

"Of course. Go on. Take Winston along. He needs some exercise."

"Okay. Thanks, Dad," she said, giving him a quick hug.

She still had to call Grant. She dialed his number, but the line was busy. While she waited, she ran to her room and grabbed a sweatshirt. Returning, she dialed his number again, and there was no answer.

In a way, Cindy felt relieved. It might be fun to go out with her friends again and have it be like old times. Then she remembered Duffy telling her to bring Grant along. Maybe it was Grant they really wanted on their volleyball team these days. They might have tried calling his house and he wasn't home, so they assumed he'd be with her. They couldn't very well call Cindy's and ask for Grant, so they'd done the next best thing and invited her along with the idea that she'd bring Grant with her.

This is silly, she thought. They're my friends, and I'm not going to waste this great day waiting for Grant to call.

"Hey, Mom," she called. "Mom!"

"They've gone to the store." Mollie appeared in the doorway of her room.

"I'm going to the beach to play volleyball. If Grant calls, tell him where we are, okay?"

"Okay." She nodded. She was deeply engrossed in *Seventeen* magazine and went back to her room as if she were in a trance. Cindy thought about leaving a note for her mom, but she knew that her dad knew where she was, and even if Mollie did space out and forget to give Grant the message, her dad would say something. With that reassurance, she raced out the door.

The volleyball game lasted until about five. Cindy had fun enjoying the beach again. The last couple weekends had been cloudy and overcast, and this was the first great day in a long time. Cindy had noticed something else, too. She enjoyed being out with all her friends, and even the volleyball game had felt more relaxed than usual. That's when she realized that there were a lot of times when she let herself get into contests with Grant even when she didn't want to. But he would suggest some activity, and her competitive spirit would just pop out. Cindy wasn't the kind of girl to back off and let anyone else win. She could respect a winner, but she would always try her hardest and would never lose on purpose for anyone's honor. She supposed it was a fault—at least that's what her sisters told her—but she couldn't help it.

After the game they sat around the campfire roasting hot dogs and marshmallows. She leaned back and enjoyed the sight of the setting sun on the water and thought how lucky she was to be growing up in Santa Barbara only a few blocks from the beach.

Cindy left for home when couples started pairing up and breaking into twosomes for romantic walks. Then she thought about Grant and for the first time wondered why he had never joined them.

Bursting through the front door, she yelled, "I'm home."

"Cindy, there you are," her mother said, coming from the kitchen and wiping her hands on a towel. "Grant's been calling here about every half hour wondering where you were. He seems quite upset, dear."

"I'll call him," she said. She ran up the stairs two at a time and pulled the phone into her room and dialed Grant's number.

"Hello," he answered. Even though she couldn't see him, she could picture his handsome face on the other end of the line. She was surprised to realize that she missed him.

"Hi, it's me."

"Nice of you to call," he said coolly.

"I just got home."

"I figured as much. I've been calling all day."

"Why didn't you join us?"

"Where were you?"

"Playing volleyball on the beach with Duffy and some of the kids. Didn't Mollie tell you?"

"I haven't talked to Mollie, and your mother didn't seem to know where you were besides doing something with Duffy."

"I'll kill her," Cindy said to herself.

"What?"

"Never mind. I'm sorry. I left a message with Mollie that I'd gone to the beach and to tell you so you could meet us there when you got home. I tried calling you before I went," she said, feeling more than a little guilty that she hadn't tried harder to reach him or at least leave a note for her mother, instead of depending on Mollie.

"Look, why don't you come over now, and we'll watch television," she said, thinking she could make it up to him.

"Well, I'm not sure I can."

Cindy felt put down by his unfriendly tone. "Well, if you want to come over, I'll be here."

"Wait a second," he said. "I'll be over around seven-thirty. Is that okay?"

"Sure."

She hung up and went looking for Mollie. Mollie wasn't in her room, however, so Cindy went into the kitchen. "Mom, where's Mollie?"

"She went to the mall with Heather about two hours ago. They were planning to do some shopping and then see a movie. Why?"

"Did she tell you that you were supposed to tell Grant where I was?" she asked, picking at the dough for the new concoction her mother was whipping up.

"No, dear. And don't eat the batter." She turned to the sink and ran water into a bowl. "All she told me was that you were somewhere with Duffy. If she said where, I missed it. Hand me that spatula, will you?"

Cindy mechanically reached for the spatula. "Well, that's great. She was supposed to tell Grant where we were, and she never said a word. Now he's mad at me. Not that I blame him," she added as she left the kitchen. After all, if she'd been the one who was waiting for him and he'd gone off without her, she'd feel pretty left out, too.

Grant arrived just before seven-thirty, and Cindy met him at the door. "Punctual, as always," she said with a smile. "You'll never guess what." She led him into the family room. "There's an old

Audie Murphy western on cable. I just love his movies, don't you?"

"Sure. That sounds okay."

Since her mother was in the kitchen testing some new recipes, her father was in his study, and Mollie and Nicole were out for the evening, they had the family room all to themselves.

Grant sprawled out on the floor, and Cindy sat near him. Winston came and settled into place between them. "This is romantic." Grant smiled. His dimple became more prominent, and Cindy could see that his resistance was wearing down.

Later they made some microwave popcorn and began tossing it into each other's mouths, trying to catch it. One piece went wailing past Cindy's mouth and smacked her in the nose. "Hey, you did that on purpose." She laughed, taking a handful of popcorn and dropping it down his shirt.

Grant spun around, grabbed her hand, and bent her wrist back so she doubled over backward. "No fair," she yelled. "I wasn't ready."

"Hey, you started this," he said, dropping popcorn into her hair and shaking the contents of the smashed popcorn from his shirt onto her face.

"What are you two doing in there?" Mrs. Lewis called.

"Nothing," Cindy said, rolling quickly to one side and spilling Grant off onto the carpet. "We'd better get this picked up before she decides to check for herself."

They quickly picked up the broken popcorn

kernels and put them in the bottom of the empty sack. Cindy leaned back and watched the movie nestled comfortably against Grant.

Near the end of the film, Mollie appeared in the doorway. She flipped on the overhead light and said, "What's everybody doing sitting in the dark? Oh, never mind," she said, backing out of the room when she saw Grant and Cindy. "Just pretend I don't even exist."

"I don't think that's possible," Cindy said to Grant. "I've been trying to pretend she doesn't exist for the last fourteen years, but every time I open my eyes, she's still there." When it came time for Grant to go, Cindy stepped out into the cool night air with him. She closed the door behind her, shutting off the light from the house. "I'm really sorry about this afternoon," she said.

He stepped closer and pulled her to him. "It's okay. I kind of overreacted. Guess I thought you were sneaking off without me and I got sort of jealous." He laughed self-consciously.

Cindy wondered if the guilt she felt showed on her face. Grant leaned down and kissed her gently. "Thanks for inviting me over tonight."

"I'm glad you came."

"So am I." He kissed her again, and then she watched as he got into his car and backed out of the driveway. As Cindy watched him go, she wondered how she could have ever thought she didn't want to be with him.

Chapter Four

At school the next day Cindy was rushing down the hall, as usual, and not looking where she was going when she smacked into someone, causing him to dump his books all over the floor. She knelt down in embarrassment and started helping him collect the scattered papers.

"I'm sorry," she said.

"It's okay."

Cindy looked at him. He had dirty blond hair and glasses, but he was kind of cute. "Hey, you're new, aren't you? Trevor, isn't it? No, Taylor. Right?"

"Yeah," he said shyly. "I guess I wasn't watching where you were going."

Cindy laughed. "I'm Cindy Lewis."

"I know."

She looked up at him in surprise and saw him

quickly turn away and begin to stack the messy papers. "You're in my biology class."

"I know, but I didn't think you knew who I was."

"A friend of mine is a swimmer at Central, and I used to watch the meets. I remember you."

"Oh," she said, feeling flattered. They were just standing up when Cindy felt a strong arm giving her a boost up.

"Lose something?"

She looked up and saw Grant towering above her. "I sort of mowed Taylor down, and I thought I ought to help him pick up the mess."

Grant eyed him critically and moved a protective arm around Cindy that made her feel claimed. "Grant, this is Taylor, um . . ." She stopped, realizing she had no idea what his last name was.

"Newcomb," Taylor supplied. "How's it going?" He put out his hand, and Grant removed his grip on Cindy to take it.

"Hi," he said. Grant seemed to relax when he realized Cindy didn't even know his last name. "We'd better get going or we'll never get a table in the lunchroom." He started steering Cindy down the hall.

"Wait a minute," she said, pulling free. "Taylor, are you going to lunch? I mean, do you want to join us?"

"No, thanks. I'm going by the library to finish up some things for an English paper. But thanks, anyway."

"How do you know him?" Grant asked as they walked toward the lunchroom.

"I don't really. He just moved here last week. I guess he saw me swim in some meet at Central, and he remembered me."

"The great jockette strikes again."

"What is that supposed to mean?" Cindy spun around to face him.

"Nothing." Grant took her arm and smiled. "Come on, there's Duffy."

When they got to the table, everyone was talking about the formal dance. Carey was telling Anna about her plans to go shopping after school that week for a dress, and if she couldn't find anything, her mother said they could go to L.A., and Anna was complaining that she could never find a dress long enough.

Duffy was telling them about some guy in his Spanish class who had rented a limo with another couple and planned to go to dinner at the country club. It didn't take long for Grant to jump in on the conversation.

Cindy couldn't believe everyone was getting so worked up over some dance. It wasn't that she didn't like dances. She'd actually enjoyed the Sadie Hawkins Dance, but this was different. It was formal. She didn't think putting on a long dress and trying to move around for four or five hours without falling on her face sounded like the kind of thing she'd always wanted to try.

Bored with the whole conversation, Cindy tuned

out her friends and began studying for her English vocabulary test next period.

After lunch, Grant walked her to class. Outside the door, he stopped and took her by the shoulders and turned her so they were facing each other. "Hey, is something wrong?"

"No. Why?"

"Well, during lunch, you were sort of quiet. It hasn't got anything to do with that Taylor guy, has it?"

"Of course not. I barely know him, Grant. It isn't like we're planning to run off together or anything. What's the matter with you?"

"Nothing," he said. "It's just that sometimes I get the feeling . . ." He let go of her. "Oh, forget it. I got to get to class."

"Okay. See you after school."

"Meet you in the quad," he said, and hurried down the hall.

Cindy watched him go and wondered why he was acting so possessive lately.

All afternoon Cindy was forced to listen to girls gushing about the dance. Didn't anyone have anything else to talk about these days?

After school, it was a relief to see Duffy and a bunch of the guys sitting around. Surely they would be talking about something more interesting. She went over, dropped her books on the table beside him, and sat on the bench below.

"What's up?" she asked, using Duffy's knee like an armrest.

"Not much. You and Grant going to the dance with anyone yet?"

"Not you, too!" Cindy groaned.

"Not me, too, what?"

"All I've heard about for the last six hours is that stupid dance. Can't we talk about something else?"

"Sounds okay by me," Duffy said, and ruffled her hair.

"What's going on here?" Grant said with mock sternness.

"Hiya, buddy," Duffy said as they slapped hands above Cindy's head. "We're just trying to figure out what else we can talk about besides the upcoming D-A-N-C-E," Duffy whispered loudly, and pointed to Cindy.

"Funny." Cindy sat up and slid over so that Grant could sit down, but instead he continued to loom above her. From the expression on his face, Cindy could tell that something was bothering him.

"So," Duffy said, his face turning as red as his hair. He pulled his leg free of Cindy's arm to stand up. "Are you and Cindy going with anyone else to the dance yet?"

"I don't know. I thought it would be sort of nice to have it just be the two of us for a change," Grant said, relaxing a little when he saw that Cindy was no longer leaning on Duffy's knee.

Cindy was confused by Grant's reaction. She thought he might be jealous but then dismissed that idea immediately. After all, Grant knew that she and Duffy were just good friends, didn't he?

"The two of you, huh?" Duffy said, raising an eyebrow.

"Come on. Grant's kidding around." Cindy jumped up and grabbed her books from the table. "We'll need all the help we can get to make it through this thing." Hoisting her books into the air, she tossed her backpack over her shoulder. "We'll see you guys tomorrow."

Grant fell into step beside her. "Do you really not want to go to this dance, or do you just not want to be with me?"

Cindy stopped in the middle of the lawn and stared at him in disbelief. "What are you talking about?"

"I know you've got this thing about dances, but I've just never known anyone so against going to a dance, that's all."

"I'm not against the dance. I'm just against having to dress up like a Barbie doll before I can get in the door!"

"You're sure that's all?"

"Of course it is. Grant, what's wrong with you?"

"Oh, nothing. Forget it." He put his arm around her and they walked out to his car. Cindy considered asking him why he'd reacted so strangely to her and Duffy but decided to leave it alone just in case she imagined the whole thing.

* * *

At home Cindy found Nicole sitting at the kitchen table reading *Bon Appétit.* Dropping her books on the table as she went by, she opened the refrigerator and asked, "Where's Mom?" as she pulled the milk carton from the shelf.

"Working, I assume." Nicole seemed engrossed in her magazine, and Cindy decided it was better not to disrupt her. Besides, Nicole would probably just tell her that she was overreacting.

She took out two slices of leftover roast beef and dropped it onto a paper towel. Turning around, she saw Nicole watching her disdainfully.

"I'll never understand how you can eat all that and still put away the food you do at the dinner table." Nicole shook her head and flipped back her shiny brown hair.

When Cindy sat down without popping off at Nicole like she usually did, Nicole looked up for the first time since Cindy had come home and set her magazine down. "Is something wrong?"

"No." Cindy picked up the roast beef and took a large bite.

"Is it Grant? Have you two had an argument or something?" A look of horror crossed her face, and she said, "You're still going to the dance together, aren't you?"

"Dance, dance, dance! Is that all you can think about? I'm so sick of hearing about it already that I'll be dead from boredom by the time the stupid thing finally gets here."

"Pardonnez-moi. It's just that I know how you

like to avoid dances. Come on, Cin, something's wrong. What is it?"

"It's just that I'll look like a freak. I know I will."

"What are you talking about?"

"Everyone else knows how to glide gracefully across the dance floor in those ridiculous high heels and long dresses. Not me. I'll stumble in and fall flat on my face. Cindy Lewis, the all-time jock who can't even put one foot in front of the other without falling down."

"Oh, come on, Cindy. I'll teach you how to walk in heels. Better yet, we'll find you a dress where you can wear little flats."

"That sounds real cute. I can't even play dress-up like everybody else."

"But that's just it; with a long dress, no one will notice your shoes."

"Until I step on the skirt of that long dress and rip a hole in it and end up losing the bottom half." Cindy got up and walked back to the refrigerator.

"And if you keep eating, you'll be able to drop by Omar the Tentmaker and pick out a nice piece of canvas and wear that."

Cindy slammed the door shut. She wasn't really hungry at all. Just nervous.

Nicole got up from the table and tucked in her blouse. "I have an idea. We'll go shopping together this weekend and find you something positively wonderful."

"I bet," Cindy said skeptically.

"Hey, didn't I help you pick out that jeans skirt?"

"Yeah," Cindy admitted reluctantly.

"And don't you like wearing it now?"

"Yeah. I guess you're right." She gave her sister a sort of half hug, dropping her arm quickly. "I've got to get started on this homework. I'll see you at supper."

Cindy left the room feeling fairly certain that they wouldn't find a dress she liked.

All through dinner Cindy listened to Mollie lamenting at the unfairness of the school in not allowing freshmen to go to the dance. Cindy finally looked up from her mashed potatoes and said, "I don't know why you're griping, shrimp. I doubt anyone would have asked you anyway."

"Cindy," her mother said in a shocked tone, "that wasn't very nice."

Cindy didn't answer.

"Well, there'll be lots of time for dances, Mollie," her father said. "In fact, one day you'll be so busy going places, you'll welcome a chance to stay at home."

"Ha," Mollie retorted.

"Play your cards right, and you can dress up as me and go with Grant," Cindy muttered.

"You're kidding!" Mollie groaned. "Aren't you just dying to go?"

"Oh, I'm dying, all right, but not to go to any stupid formal dance."

After dinner, Cindy went up to try to finish the

last of her homework. She had trouble concentrating, though. What was wrong with her? All anybody could talk about was that dance and how excited they were about it, and all she could think about was that dance and how she'd rather be baby-sitting. And she hated to baby-sit.

"This is ridiculous," she muttered, slamming her book shut. "I'm not going to spend the next two weeks being miserable about this. I'm going to put it out of my mind."

"Talking to yourself these days?" Mollie asked as she walked by. Cindy gave her a dirty look before she slammed her bedroom door shut. Then she went to her closet and looked one more time for something she might be able to wear to the dance. But it was useless. Things were the same as they'd been that afternoon. No one had slipped upstairs while she had eaten and hung a terrific-looking ball gown in her closet. "Fairy godmother, where are you?" she asked, plopping down on her bed.

Someone knocked at the door. "Phone's for you, Cindy," Mollie said. She had been so entranced in her thoughts, she hadn't even heard it ringing.

"Hello," Cindy said, picking it up and walking toward her bedroom.

"Cindy, it's me," Carey said.

"What's happening?"

"Nothing. Mom and I were just talking about when we can go shopping, and I wondered if . . ."

"Don't say it," Cindy warned. "If you called to

tell me about the dance or ask me to go shopping, hang up and call somebody else."

"What's eating you?"

"I'm sorry. Can't we talk about something else?"

"Okay. How are things between you and Grant?"

"Okay, I guess."

"What does that mean?"

"Well. He sure acted funny today."

"Funny. How?"

"Well, like, would you believe that when he came in after school this afternoon, Duffy and I were sitting in the quad like we always do, and Grant almost acted jealous of Duffy."

"How come?"

"Beats me," Cindy said, leaning back on her bed and tossing a tennis ball into the air above her head. "I was just sitting there with my arm on his knee like I've done for a hundred years, and Grant shuffles around like he's walking on hot sand in his bare feet."

"Well, what'd you do?" Carey asked.

"Nothing. I guess Duffy figured it out, 'cause he moved his leg over and stood up."

"Oh."

"I mean, can you believe it?" Cindy asked, catching the ball easily with her left hand.

"I guess I can understand how he feels."

Cindy sat up abruptly, and the tennis ball fell to the floor. "What?"

"Well, sometimes I look at the two of you, and I wonder ... I wonder whether if you and Grant broke up, he wouldn't take you out in a minute," she rushed on. "You two are just so . . ."

"Duffy?" Cindy said. "And me?" She started laughing.

"Well, what's so funny about that?"

"Duffy is my friend. Believe me, that's all it is. It's like . . . well, it'd be like going out on a date with my brother, okay?"

"Okay, I believe you. But you'd better be sure that Grant believes you. He's the one you have to worry about now."

"That's dumb. Grant doesn't have anything to worry about. And if he's stupid enough to think Duffy and I would ever have a thing for each other, that's his problem."

Nicole knocked lightly at Cindy's open door. "Hey, I'm waiting for a call," she said.

"Okay." Cindy rolled off the bed and said, "Look, I have to go. I'll see you at school tomorrow." She handed the phone to Nicole and saw Mollie standing behind her. "She's right, you know."

"Who?"

"Carey."

"Mollie, I've told you a thousand times to stop listening to my conversations."

"I couldn't help it. I heard what you said about Grant's being jealous of Duffy. I wasn't trying to listen. I was just passing by and I heard what you said. He has every right to be jealous, Cindy. After all, it's pretty hard to figure out why the girl you're supposed to be going with is always hanging around with other guys."

"What do you know about it?" Cindy asked, getting up from her bed to shut the door.

"I know enough to know that a guy doesn't understand how you and Duffy can be together all the time and call it friendship."

"Listen to the great expert on guys. Go away, Mollie. You're giving me a headache."

"I'm just trying to help." Mollie pouted.

"As if you know what love's all about." Cindy tried to shut her door on her little sister.

"For your information, I know quite a bit about love. At this very moment I happen to be very much in love with a brilliant art student who thinks I'm wonderful and sophisticated."

"Tell me about it," Cindy said with a laugh.

Mollie, always one to be dramatic, lifted her chin high and proclaimed loftily, "When you're mature enough to handle it, I will."

"If there's any growing up to be done around here, you're the one who needs it," Cindy yelled after her, and slammed the door.

Chapter Five

Early Sunday morning Cindy jumped out of bed and got straight into her gray sweats. Downstairs she gulped down a glass of orange juice and woke up Winston. Slipping quietly out of the house, she took off toward the beach, with Winston in tow. The air felt cool, and the streets were practically empty, except for those few joggers she'd meet every Saturday morning. She loved these early-morning runs. They gave her a chance to clear her head and figure things out.

Running next to the crashing waves, she nearly forgot that this was the day she and Nicole were supposed to go shopping for a formal. Maybe it wouldn't be so bad, she reasoned. Maybe she would look wonderful in the first thing she tried on, and then they could be home by noon. She sailed along the beach with Winston trailing after her. Cindy could hear his wet paws slapping the sand behind her. Every once in a while he would stop to lap at the waves or bite at a stick.

After she'd run for two miles, Cindy dropped to a rock and Winston came up and set his sandy head on her knee. She patted his head absently. "You got it made, you know that? Here you are with your fur all matted and sand in your face and no one cares. Especially you." She petted his head absentmindedly while he swept his tail back and forth in the sand.

"How come people have to be so particular about things?" He looked at her with his huge brown eyes. "Come on, dopey. Let's go home and get some breakfast," she said affectionately as she got to her feet.

When she came into the kitchen after filling Winston's dish, Nicole was already dressed and sitting at the table eating a melon. Cindy went to the fridge and took out the milk. She started to tip the carton to her lips but stopped when she caught Nicole watching her intently. Sighing loudly, she went to the cabinet and took out a glass. When she got her own place, she would drink milk straight from the carton and no one could say a thing. She'd never worry about her mom walking in or Nicole catching her in the act and looking at her as if she were thoroughly disgusting.

"Morning, sweetheart," her mother said cheerily. "How was the run today?"

"Great."

"Why don't I fix you something while you jump in the shower?" she offered. Cindy lifted her arm and took a whiff. "Is it that bad?"

"Don't be silly. You know what I mean. You and Nicole are going shopping today, and I thought you'd want to get an early start."

"Yeah, sure. If we get to the mall when the stores open, I can find something and be back here in time to catch a few waves on the beach this afternoon."

"I just can't believe a daughter of mine doesn't like shopping."

"Neither can I," said her father, coming into the kitchen and buttoning the sleeves of his shirt. "But I sure am glad when it comes time to pay the bills around here." He winked at Cindy.

"I'll be ready in ten minutes," Cindy yelled as she headed toward the bathroom. Mollie's door was closed, which meant she was still asleep. Cindy shook her head and wondered how anyone could waste such a great day.

It wasn't such a great day by the time they'd hit the fourth or fifth store. Cindy had long ago lost track of how many places they'd been. She was tired of dragging dresses back to the fitting room, and if she heard one more saleslady exclaim, "Oh, it's so much cuter off the hanger," she was going to wrap the hanger around her head.

She had tried on gowns of every color imaginable. At one store, they had picked out a black dress that made her look like some flat-chested Elvira. She had put on an awful yellow filmy thing that made her look like a Chiquita banana. Then Nicole picked out a red-and-white striped dress that made her look like a barbershop pole. Others were too short or too tight or just simply awful.

"I give up. Let's get some lunch." Cindy sighed, dropping to the bench in the fitting room. "I can't look at another thing on an empty stomach."

"Okay. Maybe after you've eaten, you'll feel better about things."

"You think so?" Cindy looked up from lacing her sneakers.

"Well," Nicole said carefully, "you actually looked nice in a couple of those dresses. I don't think you're giving it a chance. You have a negative attitude, and nothing's going to please you." She sighed.

"That's not true. Right now I would be very pleased with a large pepperoni pizza."

But by five-thirty, they still hadn't found a formal, and it was hard to tell who was more discouraged. Cindy hadn't found a thing that she liked, and although Nicole had liked several dresses, she hadn't been able to convince Cindy that they really did look nice on her.

The phone was ringing as they walked in the door. It was Grant. "What're you doing?" he asked.

"I just got in," Cindy said, then added, "I hate shopping."

"Did you find a dress?"

"Yeah, I found lots of them. It's just that none of them looked good on me."

He laughed. "I can't believe that. I've never seen you look bad in anything."

"That's because you weren't with us today."

"Well, maybe I should've been."

"Why? You need a good laugh?"

"Not as bad as you need an honest critic," he said. They talked a while longer, and when Cindy hung up the phone, she went into the family room and sat down next to her dad.

"From the look on your face, I take it the shopping expedition wasn't a success."

"Not quite. I think I'll just wear jeans and see what happens."

"You can't wear jeans," her mother reminded her. "It's a formal dance."

"I know. Maybe I'll rent a tux," she said.

The following Wednesday in Biology, Ms. Harris had the answer to Cindy's prayers. "Do you remember when I mentioned the possibility of a whale-watching expedition?" she asked the class.

Cindy felt her heart beating faster. She had been dying to see the whales ever since Ms. Harris had told them about the expedition she'd been on the year before.

"Well, I've been informed that this weekend is a perfect time to see the whales, and if we can get enough people together to charter a boat, we can go. I realize that this is short notice, and I'm sorry about this, but we'll need to go this weekend if we want to see them this year."

She went to her desk and took out a sheet of paper. "We'll have to leave at about four Saturday morning, and we'll be getting back around twelve or one Sunday morning. If you think you might be interested in going, I'd like you to sign your name on this paper. If you're not sure, put a question mark by your name."

As the sheet got closer to Cindy, she worried that there wouldn't be room for her to go. Then she worried that there wouldn't be enough people interested in going and they would have to cancel the trip. She saw that she was the tenth person on the list, and two of the signatures had question marks by them. She wrote her name. Then, remembering she still had to get out of going to the dance, added a question mark.

She passed the paper to Taylor, who was sitting behind her, and then impulsively pulled it back. "Just a minute," she told him. "I have to change something." She quickly erased the question mark and handed it back to him. Taylor smiled and added his name to the sheet.

After class Cindy saw Grant coming down the hall toward her. She went up to him, her heart racing with excitement. "Guess what!"

"What?" he said, smiling as he put his arm around her shoulders.

"Ms. Harris has arranged for us to go on a

whale-watching expedition. Doesn't that sound like fun? Would you like to go? I'm sure it will be all right," she said.

"Sure, that sounds great," he said enthusiastically.

"I knew you'd want to go. I just knew it. You'll have so much more fun than you would have had at that crazy dance, you'll see."

Grant stopped abruptly and dropped his arm. "Wait a sec. What are you talking about? *When* is this whale watching supposed to take place?"

"Saturday."

"*When Saturday*?"

"All day," she said timidly. "We leave early Saturday morning, and we'll get back late Saturday night."

"Isn't that convenient." Grant stared at her and shook his head.

"What's that supposed to mean? Hey, I can't help it if the whales are moving now and this is the best time to see them."

"Even if it means giving up the dance to be there?"

"There'll be plenty of dances in our lifetime, but this may be the last chance we ever have to see a great whale."

"Go to Sea World. They have lots of them," he said dryly.

"You're not being fair."

"Who's not being fair? How would you feel if I just suddenly canceled our date to do something else?" She opened her mouth. "No, wait, don't answer that. You'd probably be relieved, wouldn't you?"

"Come on, Grant. I never said I didn't want to be with you."

"No, but you've said enough other things."

"We'll go to the next one. I promise." She tried putting her arm through his, but he pulled free.

"I don't want to go to the next one, Cindy. I want to go to *this* one."

"Fine," she snapped. "I hope you can find someone who wants to go with you, because I'll be on a whale-watching expedition!"

Chapter Six

*On Friday night Mollie watched from the hall-*way as Cindy packed her things to leave for the whale-watching expedition. She couldn't believe Cindy could be so dumb as to not only give up a formal dance but to also give up a chance to go with someone as neat as Grant. Not only was he the cutest guy in the junior class, but he was also so great to Cindy that Mollie thought she needed a shrink.

Cindy came out of her room and set her backpack in the hallway near the door. "Well, I'm all ready to go," she exclaimed with a look of triumph.

Mollie leaned against the door and shook her head at her. "I just can't believe you're doing this."

"That's because you have no sense of adventure," she said as she went down the stairs into the kitchen. Her mother was just setting dinner on the table.

"Call your sisters, honey. We're ready to eat." Cindy turned and almost ran Mollie down.

"We're ready to eat," she told her.

"I heard," Mollie said coolly.

"Hey, Nicole," Cindy called from the foot of the stairs. "Supper's ready."

Mr. Lewis came out of the den and put his arm around Cindy as he walked her back to the kitchen. He removed his glasses and pointed them toward her bag sitting near the door. "Still going, I see."

"Of course. You don't commit to something like this and just not show up."

"Well, I believe you committed to something else, didn't you? And you don't seem too upset about not showing up there."

"That was different."

"How?"

"It was just a silly dance. This is the chance of a lifetime, to do something that will help me with my future."

"I see," he said with a slight smile.

"Well," Mollie lectured her father as she put the salad on the table, "I don't see how you can find anything funny in this. I think it's perfectly awful of Cindy to leave Grant at the last minute to run off and watch a bunch of stupid fish!"

"Shows what you know," Cindy said. "Whales are mammals."

When Mollie woke up on Saturday morning, Cindy was already gone. She still hadn't quite believed that Cindy would really go through with it. Emerging from the bathroom, Mollie heard the phone ring. She rushed to answer it.

"Hi, Mollie, it's Sarah. Want to go to the mall today?"

"Sure. What time do you want to go?"

"If we left in about an hour, my mom could give us a ride, and we can eat there."

Mollie thought longingly about all the greasy food available in the mall. It didn't fit in with her new diet, but after all, it was Saturday. She really only tried to be serious about her diet on weekdays. Weekends were meant for cheating. "Okay," she said.

She went to her room and began picking through the clothes piled on the chair and the desk, looking for her favorite sweater. She knew she'd worn it earlier that week. Where had she put it? She didn't bother looking in the drawers; she knew it wouldn't be there.

"Who was that on the phone?" her mother asked, coming into the room and setting more of her stray clothing on top of the unmade bed.

"Sarah. We're going to the mall."

"I hope you're not planning to leave too soon,

young lady, because this room is going to be cleaned up before you go."

"Aw, Mom."

"If you'd pick it up every day, it wouldn't take so long on the weekends. And if you don't start taking better care of your clothes, you won't get any new ones." She picked up a shirt from the floor. "I never even saw this on you all week."

"Oh, yeah. I was going to wear that under my blue sweater, but I liked the white one better."

"Then why didn't you hang it back up? Look at it now. It looks like it's been slept on."

"It has," she said sheepishly. She had dropped it on her bed and then forgot about it and found it the next morning.

Her mother shook her head. "Well, don't you plan to go anywhere until I see this room spotless."

Though she began grumbling almost before her mother was out of the doorway, Mollie knew there was no way out of it. She put the radio on and began cleaning and dancing at the same time. Eventually, she found the sweater she wanted to wear. It was a little wrinkled. She shook it out and then thought about giving it to her mom to throw in the dryer for a couple of minutes. That would fluff it up and make it look as good as new.

She almost started out the door when she thought better of it. After all, if she went down and asked her mom to put it in the dryer, she would have to explain how she hadn't worn it long enough for it to be dirty but she hadn't hung it up either, and she'd get another lecture on how she was going to have to learn to become more responsible. She put it in the dirty clothes hamper and decided to wear something else. She'd hardly made a dent in the pile of clothes in her room. At this rate she wouldn't get to the mall until closing.

When they finally got to the mall, Sarah and Mollie headed straight for the food to eat lunch before they did anything else. There were several kids that they knew from school there, and a couple of freshman boys from their French class invited them to sit down. Since there weren't any empty tables, the girls accepted, but Mollie thought it would have been nicer if they were older.

Sarah finished her soda and spat some of the ice at one of the boys. He retaliated by pouring a cup of ice down her back, while Moblie filled her straw and shot soda at the boy across from her. He ducked and it hit the man behind him, who didn't think there was anything amusing about a food fight in the mall.

Sarah and Mollie quickly jumped up and escaped into the bathroom in fits of laughter. They adjusted their makeup and recombed their hair while they waited for the man to leave. They were just coming out of the bathroom when Mollie saw him. Tyson Gilbert.

Mollie stopped and grabbed Sarah's arm. "Oh, my gosh. There he is."

"Who?" Sarah asked, looking around the mall.

"Don't stare," Mollie ordered, and pulled her friend around so that she couldn't see anything but the taco stand behind her.

"It's him. It's Tyson Gilbert."

"Where?" Sarah turned her head to look, but Mollie grabbed her abruptly.

"Stop that. He'll see you."

"How can he see me when I can't see him?"

"Just act cool," Mollie instructed as they walked by the table where he was sitting with some other boys. Mollie, using her most seductive and mature voice, said, "Excuse me," as she pushed by Tyson's table. Then she stopped and acted as if she'd just seen him. "Oh, hi, Tyson."

She smiled and kept walking as though seeing him were just an ordinary occurrence. Mollie swept off into the crowd and didn't catch the bewildered look on Tyson's face.

When they got around the corner, Mollie doubled over and grabbed Sarah's hand. "Isn't he just the most gorgeous guy you've ever seen?"

"I don't know. I only saw the back of his head. You kept telling me I couldn't turn around and take a better look."

"Well, of course not. You think I want him to know I'm in love with him? I have to make a plan first."

"Who is he?"

"He's just the most brilliant art student in the senior class."

"Senior? Mollie, haven't you learned your lesson about seniors yet?"

An hour or so later, they saw Tyson in the frame shop. Mollie felt her heart skip a beat as she watched him thumbing through the latest prints. She breezed into the store and began looking at the framed prints on the wall next to him. But he didn't seem to notice her.

She began thumbing through the prints in the bin next to Tyson. He looked up and smiled at her and nodded.

"Hello again," she said.

"Do I know you?" he asked. Mollie felt her cheeks flame and heard Sarah stifle a giggle behind her.

"Not directly." She smiled sweetly. "I pass you going to art every day. I'm Mollie Lewis."

"Tyson Gilbert," he said pleasantly, and then began thumbing through the prints again. "You interested in art?"

"Oh, yes," Mollie gushed. Of course she hadn't been until she became interested in him, but he didn't need to know that.

"What do you like?"

"What?" Mollie asked, feeling caught in a trap. She should have studied up before she let herself get drawn into this conversation. "Oh, everything." She waved her hand vaguely.

"I'm into realism myself. I guess it's because I like sculpting, and I really get a kick out of it when the figures become lifelike."

"Oh, me, too." She nodded quickly, relieved to be off the hook.

"Oh, you sculpt, too?"

"No," she said. "I just *like* sculpting. I've seen some of your work, and you're very good."

Now it was his turn to blush. "Thanks."

"Hey, Gilbert," a tall dark-haired boy called from the doorway. "We'd better get going. It's almost three o'clock."

"Okay. Nice talking to you . . . um . . ."

"Mollie. Mollie Lewis."

"Lewis? Any relation to Nicole?"

"She's my sister."

"She's a doll. I had French with her a couple years ago." Turning around abruptly, he left the shop, leaving Mollie looking after him, feeling her heart wilt and collapse like a shriveled flower. He hadn't even remembered her name—only her older sister—and she suspected that she'd made a total fool of herself trying to talk about things she had no idea of.

Well, she certainly wouldn't let that happen again. Filled with determination, she went straight over to the counter and asked the saleslady if they had any books on sculpture.

"I'm afraid not." The woman looked up from the picture she was matting. "We have mainly print work here and a few books on the master painters, if you'd like to see one of those."

"Thanks, some other time," Mollie mumbled. She knew what she'd do. She'd go to the library and take out some art books. The next time she ran into Tyson, she'd know what she was talking about.

Mollie was fighting to stay awake when she heard the key in the door. She hoped it was Nicole. She wanted to hear all about the dance. Instead, Cindy clambered in, knocking into things with her loaded backpack.

"How was the trip?" Mollie asked.

"It was great, but I'm too beat to talk about it tonight. I'll tell you about it tomorrow. Nicole home yet?" she asked, setting her pack down to hang up her jacket.

"No. You look a mess." Mollie frowned at Cindy's appearance. Her sister should have walked through the door in a ball gown. Instead, she was wearing jeans that were ripped at the knee and a green sweatshirt with dark stains all over it.

"So what? Wonder how the dance went." She started up the stairs. "I guess I'll have to hear about it in the morning. Good night."

Mollie watched her go up the stairs and wondered how she could be so uninterested in the dance she should have gone to. Retying her bathrobe sash, she went back into the family room to watch the rest of the *Saturday Night Movie,* but she fell asleep before it ended and only awakened when someone shut the front door. She sat up and called, "Nicole, is that you?"

"Shhh." Nicole tiptoed in, looking graceful in a

lilac silk gown. "You want to wake everybody up? Is Cindy home yet?"

"Yeah. She got in a while ago. Smelling like a fish. How was the dance?"

"It was wonderful. The decorations were gorgeous. The music was fantastic. Everyone was there."

"Poor Grant. It's too bad he had to miss it," she said, feeling even sorrier for him now.

"Oh, he didn't miss it." Nicole pulled out her french knot and shook her hair loose.

"He went to the dance? By himself?"

"No. Not by himself."

"Well, who was he with?" Mollie almost shrieked.

"Keep it down. I don't know her name. I've seen her in the halls. I think she's a sophomore."

"Oh, no. Do you think we ought to tell Cindy?"

"*Oui,* better us than someone else. But it can keep till morning. Right now I'm going to bed, and you should, too. *Bonsoir.*

But Mollie was too anxious to sleep. She went back into the family room to watch some more TV. Poor Cindy, she thought, what will she do when she finds out that Grant went without her? Then she thought again and decided that Cindy got exactly what she deserved. After all, she'd told him to go with someone else. And he had done exactly that.

Chapter Seven

Cindy rolled over and looked at the clock. It was nearly eleven o'clock. She couldn't believe it. Her parents had let her sleep in. She stretched lazily and lay on her bed thinking about the previous day. It had been thrilling watching those magnificent whales moving through the water. There was something exciting and dangerous about being so close to something so big and powerful.

She wished Grant hadn't been so stubborn and had gone with her. Oh, well, she thought, he would be sorry when she told him what he'd missed.

The phone was ringing, and she heard Mollie say, "I don't think she's up yet."

She quickly rolled out of bed. "Yes, I am. Is it for me?" Cindy called.

"Here she is." Mollie frowned and handed her the phone.

"Hello." Cindy carried the phone into her room.

"Cindy, it's me, Anna. How were the whales?"

"Awesome." Cindy fell back onto her bed.

"Awesome enough to miss the dance?"

"You bet. It was the thrill of a lifetime."

"Well, you let Grant give the thrill of a lifetime to Karie Simmons last night."

Cindy felt her throat close up. "What are you talking about?" Her hand shook.

"He took Karie to the dance. Didn't he tell you he was taking someone else?"

"No, I guess it never came up." Cindy tried acting nonchalant. "I mean, I told him to ask someone else if he really wanted to."

"I'm sorry, Cindy. I thought you already knew, or I'd have kept my mouth shut."

"It doesn't matter really. I don't own Grant, you know." Cindy laughed nervously. "And he doesn't own me. We both do whatever we want."

"You're taking this pretty well. I'd be furious."

"I would be, too, if it mattered that much. But it's no big deal," she said a lot more casually than she felt. She then asked several questions about the dance, although she couldn't have cared less. She wasn't about to let Anna know that, though, or how hurt she was that Grant could replace her so quickly. And with Karie Simons of all people. She was nearly as scatterbrained as Julie Palmer.

Setting the phone back in the hallway, Cindy

practically collided with Nicole, coming out of the bathroom. "Watch where you're going." Then Nicole's voice softened. "Who was that?" she asked, toweling off her hair.

"Anna."

"Oh. I saw her at the dance last night," Nicole said carefully. She wasn't sure whether to forge ahead and tell Cindy about Grant or to wait and see if Grant might call and tell her himself.

"She tells me that I was about the only one who missed the dance last night."

"Oh, you heard?"

"You saw him, too, then?"

"Yes. I said hi, but he spent most of the night trying to avoid me, I think."

"Well, I hope she was worth it," Cindy snapped.

"And he probably hopes your whales were worth it," Nicole retorted.

By three o'clock Cindy was restless and tired of waiting for Grant to call. Pulling on some sweats, she yelled to no one in particular, "I'm going for a run on the beach if anyone calls."

"Okay, honey," her mother called back from the kitchen. "We're eating dinner at about five, so don't be long."

Cindy went out through the garage. "Come on, boy," she called to Winston. He jumped eagerly to his feet and ran along beside her.

Sprinting to the beach, Cindy tried to run off all of her frustration. But it wasn't easy. She couldn't imagine Grant with Karie Simmons. They had nothing in common. After all, she didn't like any sports—except maybe cheerleading—if that could be considered a sport.

She imagined them sitting in some dark corner and Karie laughing and acting charming, with Grant smiling like some kind of village idiot. Karie had probably played all the silly games Julie had played when Brian took her bowling.

Grant might really eat that sort of thing up. In fact, maybe he was looking for some excuse to drop her so he could date someone else. Now that she thought about it, he had been edgy and argumentative lately. Maybe he just wanted to provoke her.

Settling down on her favorite rock, she watched the waves roll in. Winston sat beside her, but she hardly noticed him. In spite of herself, she felt tears welling up in the corners of her eyes. She reasoned that it was the wind and the salt water stinging her face, but she knew better. It was her own stupidity that was stinging her now. She jumped up quickly. "Come on, Winston, let's go home."

While Cindy pulled her sandy shoes off at the kitchen door, she heard the phone ringing. She rushed to get into the house and yell, "I've got it."

"Cindy?" She felt a pang of disappointment hearing Duffy's familiar voice. "Say, how's the Jacques Cousteau of Vista High School?"

"Tired. How about you?"

"Exhausted. We stayed out half the night, but it was a blast." There was silence on the line, and finally he said, "What's the story with you and Grant?"

"What do you mean?"

"Well, I saw him there last night, and when I tried to ask him what was going on, he said to ask you. So I am."

"I don't know," she said with a shrug. "I told him if he really wanted to go to the dance, to find someone else to take, and I guess he did."

"So are you two calling it quits or what?"

Cindy wondered why he was asking. Was he just being nice, or was there more to it? "We haven't really talked about it. In fact, we haven't talked about much of anything since last Wednesday."

"Well, if you need a little advice from the other side of things, you know you can count on me."

"Thanks, Duff." Cindy said good-bye and went to the sink to wash her hands. "Did I get any phone calls?" she casually asked her mother.

"Not that I know of," her mother said, and handed her a dish. "Put this on the table, will you?"

She should have known better than to come into the kitchen. She was always getting stuck doing little jobs. When was she going to learn to stay out of the way when her mother was preparing dinner?

Nicole breezed in, looking radiant, as usual, in

cream-colored stirrup pants and an oversized sweater that emphasized her slim figure. Comparing her to herself, Cindy looked down at her stained, stretched-out jogging pants and her T-shirt with the hole at the shoulder from an overzealous game of softball and decided that it was no wonder Grant had found someone else.

Well, that was fine with her. She tossed her head. She was who she was, and if he wanted an empty-headed flirt with just another pretty face, he deserved someone like Karie. She was glad she'd found out now instead of waiting for a year or so and finding out that's what he really wanted.

By seven-thirty that evening, Cindy knew Grant wasn't going to call. That was okay. She had decided the romance was a mistake anyhow. She'd been feeling stifled, and now he had taken the pressure off. She was free again. Free to do what she wanted without worrying about pleasing someone else. Free to talk to whomever she wanted to whenever she wanted to. But if she was so glad to be free of Grant, why did she feel so bad?

A knock at the door interrupted her thought. "Can I come in?" Nicole asked.

"Sure," Cindy said, and sat up on her bed.

"You want to talk?"

"About what?"

"Well, I just thought maybe you were feeling a little down about Grant and maybe I could help. I know how I felt when Mark and I broke up. Sometimes it makes you feel better to talk about it."

"Funny. I don't remember your talking about it at all. Anyway, there's nothing to say. Really. Grant doesn't owe me anything."

"Well, for what it's worth, he didn't look like he was having a very good time last night."

"Too bad. I had a great time. He should have come with me," she added sarcastically.

"Maybe if you called him," Nicole suggested.

"What for? He knew what I was doing. I'm not the one who sneaked out behind his back."

"Cindy, you're the one who refused to go with him. Canceled at the last minute. Remember? He was probably just hurt and trying to get back at you."

"Well, it didn't work, because I don't care. If that's all I mean to him, let him have Karie. They deserve each other." Cindy flipped over onto her stomach and hugged her pillow.

"Cindy Lewis, you are too stubborn to believe." Nicole got up and went to the door. "But even if you are stubborn, I'm here if you want to talk."

"Thanks, but I'm just fine."

And she was, until she turned out the lights and the darkness enveloped her and she had to turn her face to the wall and cry.

Cindy couldn't tell if it was real or imagined, but the next day at school it felt as if people were staring at her and saying things about her when she'd walked by. A couple of times she was sure people changed the subject when she walked up to join them in a conversation.

On her way to lunch, she finally saw Grant for the first time that day. He was coming down the stairs. He smiled and waved to her, but suddenly flustered, Cindy decided to play it cool and pretend not to see him. Then she realized it wasn't she he was smiling at. Karie Simons was walking toward him. He stopped to talk to her. Cindy figured either he hadn't seen her, or he'd chosen to ignore her. Well, two could play at that game. She'd ignore him as well.

He moved off down the hall, and someone came up behind her and put an arm around her shoulders. "Buck up, little soldier," Duffy said. "The recruits are restless, but the war ain't lost yet."

"Duffy, what does that mean?" she asked him.

"Beats me, but it sounded like the kind of thing John Wayne would have said at a time like this."

"You're crazy; you know that?" She laughed for the first time in two days.

"Yep. And I'm also hungry. Join me in the cafeteria?" he asked, and extended his hand in front of her to lead the way.

"Don't mind if I do, Duke."

Cindy waited for Grant to call her and at least let her know that he was through with her, but he never called. She almost called him several times to tell him that she didn't want to see him anymore but then decided that that might be kind of dumb, since he obviously wasn't seeing her anymore anyway.

She was sitting in the family room when Mollie came in with a bowl of ice cream. "Thought you were on a diet," Cindy said.

"I am, but I thought this might settle my stomach."

"You sick?"

"Not really. I think it's just love."

"Not again." Cindy groaned.

"This time it's different," she said dreamily.

"Who's the lucky guy?" Cindy said, not really wanting to know but feeling compelled to say something.

"I doubt you know him. He doesn't exactly hang out in your circle of friends." She took a bite of her ice cream. "He's an artist. His name is Tyson Gilbert."

"You're right. I don't know him. Where did you meet him?"

"We're in the art club together."

"Art club?" Cindy said with a laugh. "Since when did you become interested in art?"

"Since I met Tyson. I've discovered the beauty of good art and music."

"That's what I've been hearing on your stereo? What is that junk anyway?"

"That junk, as you call it, happens to be classical music by great composers like Beethoven and Bach."

"Well, where did *you* get it?"

"At the library."

"Take my advice, Mollie. Be yourself. You can get in a lot of trouble trying to make yourself over into something you're not."

"You're a great one to be giving advice about anything having to do with love."

"I'm just trying to help," Cindy said, getting off the couch and leaving the room.

"Well, if you help me the way you help yourself, I'll have a lot to look forward to," Mollie called after her. "Like being an old maid."

Chapter Eight

Mollie passed Grant in the hall on Monday. Though he said hello, he was far from his usual friendly self. Maybe it was because he was walking with Karie. Mollie took one look at Karie's long strawberry-model-thin figure, blond hair, and stylish clothes and thought, Poor Cindy, how could she ever hope to compete with that?

Sure, Cindy had been a challenge at first, but a guy didn't want to keep getting beaten over the head with a girl's ability to outdo him in so many things. And independence and self-assertiveness could get to be a drag when they took over a relationship.

She stood rooted to the ground and watched them walk down the hall. At least he didn't have his arm around her or anything. Just then someone hit her arm and her books scattered. She knelt to pick them up and looked right into Tyson Gilbert's blue eyes.

"Sorry," he apologized.

"That's okay."

"Hey, I met you the other day, didn't I? You're a Lewis, right? Wait, don't tell me." He hesitated a minute, and just as she was about to supply the answer for him, he said, "Mollie!"

"Right," she said, breaking into what she hoped was an irresistible smile. Well, she hadn't bowled him over with her charm, but at least he remembered her name.

She reached out to retrieve her English homework just as someone stepped down on it. The paper gave way, splitting into two uneven parts. She took the pieces into her lap and tried to iron out the wrinkles with her hand.

"Oh, man, I'm sorry," he said. "Was that something important?"

"No." She lied. It was only due next period, but why make him feel worse?

"Look, I got to get going." He got to his feet. "I have a class now."

"Me, too." As he turned to leave, she said, "Will you be at the meeting after school?"

"The art club meeting? Yeah, will you?"

She nodded.

"I didn't know you were a member."

"I just joined."

"Then I'll see you there. Look, I got to run. Sorry about your paper."

"No big deal."

Sarah came up behind her after he'd left. "Mollie, was that who I think it was?"

"Yes," she said, trying not to smile.

"What were you talking about? What did he say?"

"Not much. He sort of ran into me, and he stopped to help me pick things up."

"Do you think it was an accident? Maybe he did it on purpose."

"I don't think so." But she started to smile as she considered the possibility.

Sarah took Mollie's arm and started pulling her toward the stairs. "Come on. You're going to be late to class."

Mollie sat in English and rewrote her homework while she thought about what Sarah had said. Maybe Tyson had meant to run into her? After all, he had remembered her name.

"Miss Lewis?" Ms. Nisson said.

"Yes?"

"Well?"

"Well, what?" she asked, feeling her face turn bright red.

"Do you know why the doctor refused to treat the infant early in the story before they found the pearl?"

"Um . . ."

"Did you read the assignment?"

"Yes, but I . . ." Darn, she knew the answer to this. She just needed time to think. By the time she had put her thoughts in order, Ms. Nisson had moved on to someone else. Mollie realized her academic future looked pretty bleak if she didn't start concentrating and stop daydreaming in class.

Mollie sat at the back of the room and listened to Tyson and a few others plan the decorations for the upcoming open house for the PTA. He was heading the committee for the cafeteria decorations and asked for volunteers. Several people raised their hands, and Tyson selected five kids. Mollie took it as a good sign that she was one of them.

After the meeting, Tyson met with them briefly and told everyone they would begin making the decorations after school in a few days. Mollie was ready to begin now. Seeing him every day—outside of school—she just knew she'd get a chance to get to know him a lot better. Maybe she could get him to drive her home or, better yet, take her to Pete's, where everyone could see the two of them together.

At home Mollie watched Cindy's situation grow steadily worse. She didn't know how much longer everyone could live with it. Mollie found herself jumping for the phone every time it rang and hoping that it would be Grant calling for Cindy. Cindy wasn't the easiest person to live with when things were okay, but when they were bad, she was almost unbearable. Both Mollie and Nicole had done their best to avoid her. But it wasn't easy. She was always at home these days.

One afternoon Mollie had suggested that Cindy go to the beach because she had heard Duffy tell a bunch of kids that he and Grant would be there after school. Cindy, who was usually at the beach every day, said she had to stay home and study. That was when Mollie knew that Cindy was really in a bad way. Cindy had never done so much studying before.

Toward the middle of the week, Cindy came in and savagely threw her backpack into the chair in the entry. "I hate him," she said vehemently, storming into the kitchen.

"Who?" Mollie asked, assuming she must mean Grant.

"Duffy! How could he be so dumb?"

"What did he do?"

"He asked me to meet him in the quad after school, and when I got there, he had Grant sitting beside him, and he expected me to march right up to them and butt into the conversation."

"Maybe that was the whole idea. To get you and Grant talking again."

"Well, it's a stupid idea if that's what he's trying to do. I have no intention of running after Grant MacPhearson. He knows my phone number. He can call me."

She grabbed her books and went to her room, slamming the door behind her. Mollie watched her go and then went to the phone in the kitchen and dialed Grant's number.

"Hello," he answered.

"Grant? It's Mollie Lewis."

"Yes?" he said, distantly polite.

"I was just wondering how you've been. It's been a while since we saw you around here."

"Talk to your sister about that," he said coldly. "She was the one who wanted to do her own thing."

"I don't know if that's what she really wanted."

"Well, it's what she got."

"Yeah, well, I was wondering if you might want to drop by tomorrow and . . ."

"Look, Mollie, I know what you're trying to do. Cindy knows my number. If she wants to clear things up, she can call me. But I'm not holding my breath."

"Okay, then, I guess I'll be seeing you at school, huh?"

"Yeah," he said. The line went dead, and Mollie wondered how the two of them would ever work things out. They were both so stubborn. It was clear *she* would have to do something about it.

Heather sat across from Mollie at Taco Rio and listened as she told her about the way Cindy had loused up her life with Grant. "I just can't believe she'd do anything so dumb," Mollie said. "And all because of having to wear some stupid long dress." She helped herself to Heather's nachos.

"I can tell you this much," she continued. "If

Tyson and I get together and he wants me to wear a parka and sit on the beach while he sculpts seagulls, I'll follow along behind him and carry his clay."

"That's the difference between you and Cindy, though. Two extremes. Cindy's more practical."

"And she told me I had no sense of adventure," Mollie went on. "Well, I have a lot more adventure in my soul than she has romance in hers." Mollie's eyes lit up. "I just got a brilliant idea. Let's give her a little adventure and romance all rolled up into one."

"What are you cooking up now?" Heather asked suspiciously.

"You know where the scene shop goes back to the tool area and there's that closet with the locking cabinet in it?"

"You mean the old janitorial closet?"

"That's the one," Mollie said, leaning forward and getting very excited. "Well, I just happen to have a key to that closet. I borrowed it once during the *Grease* rehearsals, and I forgot to give it back. Well, I didn't really forget. Actually, I lost it, but—"

"Okay, Mollie, get on with it," Heather interrupted. "Just what do you plan to do with a key to the janitorial closet?"

"Unlock it, of course," she said trumphantly, popping a nacho into her mouth.

"Big deal," Heather said, leaning back in the

booth and feeling disappointed in her friend's imagination.

"And then lock it again."

"Yeah, that sounds like real fun, Mollie."

"But the fun will be that when we lock it up, Cindy and Grant will be inside, and they'll have some time alone to iron out all their problems."

"Are you kidding? How did you ever come up with such a crazy idea?"

"Actually, I saw it on *All My Children,* only the wrong people got locked in the cellar, and Erica fell in love with Jeremy instead, but it doesn't matter—the plan worked."

"I'm not sure it will work for Grant and Cindy."

"Why not? The biggest problem is that they aren't speaking to each other and both of them are too stubborn to admit they're wrong."

Heather nodded.

"So what better way to get them to talk things out than to trap them together and not let them come out until they're talking again?" Mollie concluded.

"Mollie, you're amazing," Heather said with a mixture of admiration and exasperation. Then her face fell. "But Cindy and Grant don't have anything to do with the theater department. How are you going to get them down to the tool room?"

"I'll have to talk to Grant, and you talk to Cindy," she said.

"But what will we say?"

"Let's see. What sounds logical?" Mollie twirled

her straw as she sat, deep in thought. "I got it! The coach needs to adjust something in the gym, and he needs to borrow a wrench from the theater department."

"Why not just ask the custodian?"

"I don't know." Mollie frowned impatiently. "Maybe no one's down there, and he needs it right away, and so he called the theater room and they said he could send someone down there."

"Right," Heather said, thinking that Mollie might pull it off. "When should we arrange for this meeting?"

"The sooner the better. The longer this thing drags on, the more they will have to fight over when they finally do get together."

"I can't take too many more weeks like this one. Cindy is so touchy that she flies off the handle at everyone. If this doesn't work, I'm going to put her up for adoption or rent her out as a foster kid to some needy family."

Chapter Nine

Heather was waiting in the hall for Cindy on Thursday afternoon. "I'm so glad I caught you." Heather ran up to her. "The coach sent me to find you to see if you could get a wrench from the theater department. Actually, he asked me to get it, but I'm going to miss my ride if I go, and I know you have practice, so you'll see him. Could you do it?"

Cindy shifted her weight restlessly from one foot to the other. "I don't even know anything about the theater department, Heather. How am I supposed to find a wrench down there?"

"Well, there's a tool cabinet at the back of the stage where the scene shop is. I'm sure someone's down there. Just go and look for the tool cabinet to the right of the door."

"Okay," Cindy said with a sigh.

"Thanks a lot," Heather said.

Cindy watched her going off down the hall and turned around and went back toward the theater. She hated snooping around in strange places.

She stepped into the darkened auditorium. "Anybody here?" she called. No one answered. She looked up on the stage and thought she saw a light coming from the back of the stage area. She climbed up on the stage and went behind the curtain. The door to a small room about the size of a walk-in closet was open, and the light was on inside.

In the room she saw that the cabinet was padlocked. Hearing someone in the doorway behind her, she jumped.

"What are *you* doing here?" Grant asked.

She spun around and said, "Getting a wrench for the coach. What ... oh, wait a minute ..." Before she could say any more, the door slammed shut and Cindy heard someone snap a lock in place. She heard scuffling feet and knew before she even tried the door that they were locked in.

Grant turned quickly and pushed against the door. He tried forcing it open but soon saw that it was no use. "This is real cute. Did you arrange it?"

"Me? Why would I do something this stupid?"

"Well, obviously the door didn't just close by itself."

Cindy pushed past him and began banging on

the door and yelling, "Mollie Lewis, you come back here and unlock this door."

"Mollie?" Grant asked. "I should have known when she called the other day that she was up to something."

"She called you?"

"Yeah. I can't believe I'm so dumb. I should have known. Even after all that, I let her talk me into coming down here to borrow a nonexistent wrench." He leaned against the door and let himself slide easily to the floor.

"Are you just going to sit there?" Cindy demanded, hand on hip.

"Got any suggestions, Wonder Woman? Perhaps you'd like to knock the door down? I'd be happy to move out of the way."

"You are such a . . . a creep!" Cindy stamped her foot and glared down at Grant.

"I'm a creep?" he said, getting to his feet.

"That's what you call someone who does creepy things," she retorted.

"And just what did *I* do?"

"I can't even believe you can ask me that. Why, you're looking for any chance you can to make me look bad."

"Come on, Cindy. You're way out in left field. What did I do to make you look bad?"

"For one thing, you insisted that I go to that stupid formal dance when you knew I'd look like a dope in a long gown."

"That's all in your head, Cin," he said, sitting

back down on the floor and resting his hands on his knees. Then he looked up at her and smiled. "Besides, you'd look great in anything."

She felt herself beginning to cool off, but couldn't help asking, "Better than Karie?"

"I'll have to think about that one," he teased. Then he saw the look on her face and could see she wasn't in any mood to be teased. "Better than anybody."

She smiled. "Come here," he said and she slid to the floor beside him.

"How were the whales?" he asked, putting his arm around her.

"Pretty good. How was the dance?"

"Okay." She leaned her head back and he kissed her. There was definitely something romantic about being locked in a smelly old tool closet. They sat like that for a while, and Cindy enjoyed the nearness of Grant again.

"This is nice," he said softly into her hair. "If you hadn't been so hardheaded, we could have made up a week ago."

"Me?" she said, leaning away from him. "I didn't go out with someone else."

"You told me to."

"Since when do you do everything I tell you to?"

"I always have. That's been the trouble with our whole relationship. You always have to have things your way. When we go anywhere, it has to be where you want to go. When we do anything, it has to be your idea."

She got to her feet. "That's not fair, Grant. I do lots of things I don't want to do to make you happy."

"And I do things I don't want to, to make you happy."

"Well, let's make each other happy from now on and not see each other anymore."

"Sounds good to me," he said angrily, pulling on the doors of the tool cabinet.

"What are you doing?"

"Trying to get this open."

"What for?"

"I'm going to get a hammer."

"Why?"

"After I get it, I'm going to bust the door down and get out of here before we kill each other."

"That's great. On top of everything else, you're a vandal, too."

"Just shut up. It was your stupid sister who got us into this in the first place."

"Mollie is not stupid. She was only trying to help. But obviously she had no idea how obstinate you can be."

"Oh, that's good. Coming from you, the queen of obstinance." He had nearly gotten the tool cabinet open when the door suddenly opened, revealing Heather standing there looking at them.

"I'm sorry. Someone must have accidentally

shut the door and locked it without realizing anyone was in here."

"Save it," Grant said, pushing her aside.

"Where's Mollie?" Cindy asked, storming out after Grant. Heather watched them go their separate ways and decided the plan didn't always work in real life as well as it did in the movies.

Cindy moved through the halls of the school promising herself she would strangle Mollie when she found her. Spying Sarah near the cafeteria, she called, "Have you seen Mollie?"

"She was supposed to be making decorations for the open house with the art department."

Propelled by her anger, Cindy ran up the stairs two at a time. In the art room, she looked at the students sitting around the tables. "Is Mollie Lewis in here?" she asked, trying to sound a lot calmer than she was feeling.

"She went outside a few minutes ago," a cute blond boy told her. Cindy wondered if he was the reason for Mollie's recent fascination with the art world. Right now, though, she was more concerned about ending her little sister's fascination with *her* love life.

Cindy went into the quad and looked around for Mollie. Duffy hailed her over, and she called out, "I've got to do something first."

Duffy jumped off the table and came toward her. "Hey, Lewis. Are you avoiding me?"

"Of course not, but right now I have to find Mollie. I'll be back."

"What do you want with Mollie?" he asked curiously.

"I'm going to kill her."

"Oh." He laughed. "How come?"

"It's a long story. Just tell her I'm looking for her if you see her around."

Checking the various exits of the school, she finally spotted a lone figure huddled against the steps outside the theater door. Figures, Cindy thought. I should have looked there first. Mollie couldn't resist sticking around to see how her plan worked out. Well, if she'd been listening at the door, she'd heard plenty.

Cindy stalked over to her. "I'm going to kill—" She stopped short when she realized that Mollie was crying. "What's wrong?" she asked, startling Mollie, who jumped at the sound of her voice.

She tried to hide her face, and Cindy sat on the step below her. "Okay, so it didn't work. You don't have to cry about it."

"But I thought he liked me," Mollie half whispered.

Cindy, assuming Mollie had heard Grant telling her that Mollie was stupid, said, "He didn't mean it."

"How do you know?" She sniffed.

"Because I know him."

"You know Tyson?" Mollie looked up at Cindy.

"Tyson? I thought we were talking about Grant."

"Grant? Whatever gave you that idea?"

"Nothing," Cindy said.

"Why do you think he picked me to be on his

committee and ran into me in the hall if he didn't like me a little?"

Dazed, Cindy shook her head and said, "I don't know."

"See, when I met him at the mall, he seemed interested, and then when he let me be part of his committee, I thought sure it was because he wanted to get to know me better, and that wasn't it at all," she said as she pushed a strand of long blond hair away from her face.

"What in the world are you talking about?" Cindy finally asked.

"Tyson," she said emphatically. "I went into the back room and saw him holding Celia Armstrong's hand, and they were laughing and talking with each other and didn't even notice me come into the room. I feel like such a fool. Why would he ever be interested in me?"

"Is Tyson the artist you're interested in? He's a senior, right?"

Mollie nodded.

"Mollie, don't put yourself down; you're a cute kid—"

"I'm *not* a kid," Mollie interrupted.

"Yes, you are," Cindy went on. "That's the problem. You don't see yourself as one, but you're not senior material yet. Why not be a little more realistic? I'm sure there are a lot of freshmen and sophomores who would love to go out with you."

"You think so?" She sniffed.

"I'm sure of it."

"Oh, Cindy, sometimes you're really nice."

"And most of the time you're a real pain."

Mollie looked up abruptly.

"Like when you try stupid stunts like locking Grant and me in the tool closet."

"Oh, that. It didn't work, huh?"

"No, it didn't. It made things a lot worse. If Heather hadn't come along when she did, we might have killed each other. So I'd appreciate it if you stop being a busybody." She got to her feet. "Face it, this is just not the year for the Lewis sisters to be in love."

"Oh, Cindy, what a depressing thought," Mollie wailed.

"Come on, I'm late for practice, and you should get home."

"My books are in the art room." She stopped and put her hands to her face. "Oh, Cin, I can't go in there like this. I must be a mess."

She was right. Her face was all blotchy and red, and it was obvious she had been crying. "I'll get them for you. The only thing worse than crying over some guy is letting him see you do it."

"Thanks, Cindy. I owe you one."

"Will it do any good?"

"What?"

"If I asked you to stop meddling in my life, could you do it?"

"Probably not."

Cindy messed up the back of her little sister's long hair. "I didn't think so."

Chapter Ten

At lunch the next day Cindy joined Anna, Carey, and Duffy at their table. She sat down beside them and opened her lunch to see what she had. She actually didn't feel like eating, but she wasn't the type to stop eating for anybody.

"Hey, Cindy, we're going to the movies tonight. Want to come?" Carey asked in between bites of her tuna sandwich.

"Yeah, that'd be fun," Cindy said, grateful that she wouldn't have to spend another Friday night in the house with her parents.

It didn't used to be like that. She always had places to go with her friends; but lately, it seemed as if they were all pairing off to do things. She felt like a fifth wheel when she tagged along. All this hadn't bothered her very much when she was going out every Friday night, too.

Duffy reached over and took her banana. "Are you going to eat this?" he asked.

"Not now," she said, watching him peel it.

"Good. Mind if I do?" He had already bitten into it.

"Go ahead," she said with a grin, which faded quickly when she heard a familiar voice behind her. "Hi, guys, what's up?"

Cindy didn't turn around. She didn't have to. She knew it was Grant. He sat down on the other side of Anna and nodded coldly to Cindy; she nodded back. Cindy noticed the look Duffy gave Carey.

"Well, I have to get to my locker before class starts." Cindy got up and climbed off the bench.

"You still have five minutes," Duffy said as Carey nudged him in the ribs.

"I'm having trouble with my combination," she lied.

"See you," Grant said as she passed him.

"Yeah, see you," Cindy said.

Just as she neared her locker, she saw Taylor coming around the corner. "Hi," he said. "Where you headed?"

"English."

"Man, that test over *Julius Caesar* is a tough one."

"Have you had it already?" she asked. "That's a

dumb question. Of course you have, or you wouldn't know if it's hard."

"Just be sure you get it straight about who was in on the assassination plot, and there are some quotes from some of the major characters."

Cindy had read the whole thing, but she hadn't felt that any of it had sunk in. Shakespeare was so boring. Everything was boring lately. She couldn't wait until this lousy school year was over.

"Well, I suppose I'd better get to class. Thanks for the information," she said.

"No problem. Hey," he said. She stopped at the door and turned back to him.

"Yeah?"

"Are you busy Friday night?" He nervously stuffed his hands into his pockets and looked down at the floor.

"Yes, I am."

"Okay. Some other time, then." He began backing down the hall toward his classroom, and Cindy felt guilty. Maybe she should invite him to go along with everyone else. After all, what was one more person? But then it might seem like a date. She wasn't sure she was ready to date anyone. But Taylor was nice. They'd had a fun time on the whale-watching trip, but she'd gotten the feeling then that he liked her a bit too much. She didn't really know how to react to boys' interest. So far, there had been only Grant.

* * *

Cindy grabbed her jacket and rushed down the stairs. "I'm leaving now," she called. Duffy had been waiting patiently in the car for the last five minutes.

He got out and let her in. She climbed into the backseat between two guys from the water polo team, Mike and Jason. Anna, Duffy, and Carey were in the middle of a conversation about a government test. Cindy looked out the window and watched as the streets of Santa Barbara rushed by.

They passed another car, and Mike leaned forward to yell something out the window. Cindy watched while Jason climbed over the top of her to get a better look at the girls in the next car. At the red light, Jason rolled down the window and yelled, "Where are you girls headed?"

Neither of them answered. They just turned to each other and laughed. "You need company?" Mike yelled.

"Looks like you already have some company," the girl on the passenger's side said.

Mike looked back at Cindy, who was trying to melt into the seat. "Who, her? Aw, this is my little sister." He hit her playfully on the head, and Cindy retaliated by ramming her knuckle into his thigh. "Ow!" he yelled.

The light turned green, and they drove away. "Hurry up and catch them," Jason said. "I think they liked us."

Cindy wondered if everyone reached puberty

and their brains fell out. She had known these guys since junior high, and they had acted more mature then than they did now. All they ever seemed to talk about these days was which girl had the best legs and who looked the greatest in a given day. Cindy settled back into the seat between them.

"Come on, Cin, lighten up," Mike nudged her.

"I am," she snapped.

"I can see that," Duffy said, looking at her in the rearview mirror.

"Who asked you?" Cindy said.

Cindy moved down the aisles looking for her friends. The movie had already started, and she had been elected to wait in line for popcorn. She balanced three large cartons carefully as she dodged people in the aisle. "Excuse me. Excuse me," she said while she stepped over everyone's feet.

"Have any trouble finding us?" Carey whispered.

"Not really. You're pretty easy to hear." She nodded toward Mike and Jason, who were laughing and making crude comments about the upcoming movie.

"They can act like such animals," Anna whispered. Cindy thought back to the time when she would have been between them yelling things at the screen, too. More than once someone had gotten up and moved because she and a bunch of guys were making too much noise.

The previews had just started when Cindy turned to talk to a girl behind her that she knew from Spanish class. She turned back around, and there were two people sitting in front of her. A tall head was blocking her view. She leaned toward Anna. "How come I always get the tall ones?"

Anna had a funny look on her face and didn't say anything, just smiled. The boy put his arm around the girl, and she leaned her head toward him. That was a little better. At least it left a hole she could see through.

Just when she had adjusted, he moved his arm, and the girl sat up again. Cindy bobbed her head the other way. "Here, trade me places," Cindy asked Anna.

When she got up, she accidentally bumped the boy in front of her with the popcorn box, spilling some of it down his shirt. "I'm sorry," she said.

He turned around and said, "That's okay." Then they both froze. It was Grant. She quickly sat down in Anna's seat, a silly smile frozen on her face. She didn't enjoy the movie much after that. She kept finding herself staring at Grant and trying to see if he was holding Karie's hand. When he said anything to her, Cindy wondered what he was saying.

In the middle of the movie, she got up and went into the bathroom. She looked at herself critically in the mirror. She had probably been right in her hunch that Grant had been looking for an excuse to break up with her.

Karie Simmons was more his type. She was not only a cheerleader; she was feminine and pretty and all the things guys liked in a girl. She was more like a girlfriend than a friend who happened to be a girl.

"You okay?" Carey asked. Cindy looked up into the mirror and saw her reflection as she stood behind her.

"Sure. I just had to use the bathroom."

"Me, too," Carey said, going to the sink. "I don't think he saw us when he sat down, do you?"

"Who?" Cindy asked. "Oh, Grant? Who knows?" She picked up a paper towel and wiped her hands. "We're probably missing the best part."

She went out of the bathroom, and Carey followed her. Carey obviously hadn't needed to use the bathroom any more than Cindy had.

After the movie, Duffy suggested they stop for a pizza. Cindy, having a feeling that Grant and Karie would probably go to Pete's, suggested Taco Rio instead. Duffy, always easy to get along with, turned the car toward Taco Rio.

Biting into a large burrito supreme, Cindy thought it tasted bland. She took the hot sauce from the table and squeezed the bottle. Nothing came out. There was lots of dried food in the opening, and she tried to unscrew the top, but the lid was stuck on too tight for her to budge it.

"Here, let me try that," Jason offered. He turned the bottle upside down and began to squeeze. Nothing happened. He pointed it at Cindy and squeezed again, making a machine-gun sound. Suddenly the clogged opening broke free and sauce began to squirt out all over Cindy's face.

Anna hit Jason's arm, causing a line of sauce to run down the front of Cindy's sweater. Cindy, who had closed her eyes against the onslaught of hot sauce, felt someone press a napkin into her hand.

She wiped her face, but all she did was smear the sticky sauce around on her face. Reaching blindly for another napkin, she felt her arm bump into something and heard a crash.

"Oh, look, isn't that . . ." she heard someone say. Then there was the sound of something falling. Cindy heard Grant's familiar voice.

"Oh, geez." She opened one eye and saw him sitting on the floor.

"Are you okay?" Karie asked. She glared at Cindy and helped him to his feet.

"I'm fine." He looked down at his wet jeans. "I just wasn't planning on going ice skating tonight." He kicked a piece of stray ice out of his way while Cindy looked down at the plate in front of her. When she finally looked up, Grant and Karie were gone.

Duffy smiled. "Atta way to go, Lewis. Knock him off his feet."

Chapter Eleven

Mollie took her latest disaster out of the kiln and looked at it in despair. Why didn't things turn out the way she wanted them to? In her head she saw all these perfect images, but once she started molding the clay and trying to sculpt them with her tools, they began to take on a shape of their own.

She wrapped the blob in a paper towel and slid it into her purse. "What are you hiding?" She jumped, causing her purse to fall to the floor. The towel opened, and the sculpture lay on the floor in several pieces.

"Gee, I'm sorry." The blond boy knelt down to pick it up.

Mollie knelt down beside him. "Don't be. It

looks better this way." She put the pieces in the garbage.

"Hey, give it time."

"I have."

"Have you thought about trying something else?" he asked.

"Like what? Home Ec?"

"No." He laughed. "Have you ever thrown a pot?"

"A glass once or twice when one of my sisters got out of control, but not any pots that I can remember."

He laughed again. He put out his hand then withdrew it when he saw it was covered in clay. "I'm David Stevenson," he said, wiping his hand on his jeans.

"Mollie Lewis."

"I've seen you around here quite a bit lately. Are you in an art class?"

"No, I just decided I wanted to see how I liked art before I got locked into a semester course."

"That's smart."

But Mollie wasn't listening. She was looking over his shoulder at Tyson, who had just entered the room. David looked around to see what was so interesting. "I see the attraction now," he said softly.

"What?" she asked, looking back at him.

"Nothing. I have to finish cleaning up. If you ever want a lesson on the potter's wheel, look me up."

"Thanks, I will."

Mollie adjusted her blouse beneath her belt and ran her fingers through her hair. She went over to Tyson and looked at the piece he was unwrapping. He put the damp cloth on the table and picked up one of his tools.

Mollie studied the dolphin he was working on and marveled at the perfection of the piece. "You're amazing," she said genuinely. "I don't know how you do it."

Tyson smiled up at her. "Hi, Mollie. How's your piece coming?"

"It isn't."

"Why not?"

"It fell to its death a few minutes ago."

"Oh, really. That's too bad," he said. He bent over, engrossed in his work again.

"You wouldn't say that if you'd seen it." He smiled. She rested her chin on her hand and watched him work. She studied the intensity on his face. She wished she had that kind of commitment. That kind of talent. Tyson would be a lot more attentive to her if she could make things like that.

"Hi, there." Celia came up behind them. She set her books down next to Tyson and sat on the stool beside him.

"Hi," Tyson said, looking up briefly.

"It's looking good," she said.

"Thanks."

Tyson was so absorbed in his work that Mollie

could stare at him without his noticing her. She watched his auburn hair catch the light as he tilted his head from side to side to get a better angle on his work. Once in a while he would frown at something he felt wasn't coming along the way he wanted it to. Then there were those moments when a smile would flash on his face and his eyes would sparkle with pleasure. He was the best-looking boy she knew. Maybe it was not just his looks that made him attractive. There was so much more to him. Mollie had never known anybody with so much talent and dedication before.

Mollie looked up and caught Celia staring at her. She stood up and said, "I guess I should be going."

"Okay. See you, Mollie," Tyson said absently, not even looking up.

She went to the other side of the room to get her books. Turning around, she saw Celia put her arm around Tyson and pull him toward her. With her thick mass of black curls, heavy eyebrows over dark brown, almost black eyes, and pale, perfect skin, Celia looked like a gypsy and an artist, Mollie thought. They were perfect for each other.

She stopped outside the door to rearrange her books, which had begun to slide. That's when she heard Celia say, "She has a case on you, you know?"

"Mollie?" Tyson said in disbelief.

"Yes."

"You're crazy. She's just a kid."

Mollie squeezed back the tears and rushed quickly down the hall. She pushed open the door to the girls' bathroom and examined her face in the mirror above the sink. She *was* a kid. The girl looking back at her still had the face of a child. Cute—but definitely not exotic. She turned sideways and looked at her profile. There was nothing wrong with her face, and she knew she had pretty eyes, but she could never compete with someone like Celia.

She wiped the tears from her face and grabbed her books before going out the door. She pushed the door open and heard someone on the other side go "Ooof."

Mollie grabbed the door and stepped into the hall. David was standing on the other side of the door. "I'm sorry," she said. "Are you hurt?"

"No, I'm okay." He stepped out from behind the door and noticed her red eyes. "Hey, are *you* all right?"

"Yeah," she said, touching her puffy eyes. "I must have gotten some dust or something in my eyes. They started watering like crazy. I came in here to wash them out."

"Can you see?"

"Sure. I'll go home and use some Visine."

"Where do you live?"

She told him her address, and he said, "I live a

couple of blocks from there. I'll walk you home to be sure you get there safely."

"Okay," she said, feeling happy for the company.

As they walked, David told her he'd moved to Santa Barbara from Colorado. His father had been transferred, and they hadn't really had any choice. He liked California, but it was certainly different from Colorado. He missed his friends, and mostly he missed skiing. He was a good talker, and Mollie felt comfortable listening to him.

"Guess it was kind of tough to leave, huh?"

"Was it ever. My brother, Todd, wouldn't come at all. He stayed in Colorado with his best friend. Not that I blame him. He's a senior, and it's pretty tough to leave all your friends and move away to a new school the semester before you graduate.

"My folks kept telling me it shouldn't be that hard for me to adjust. In Colorado, ninth grade is still considered junior high. So a lot of my friends were split up to different high schools this year anyway. I was still getting the feel of things when we moved."

"I know what you mean," Mollie said, remembering the pain she had felt at the beginning of the year when she had been separated from Arlene and all her junior high friends. She'd been the only one in her group who had been assigned to Vista.

"Well, this is my house," Mollie said. "Thanks for walking me home."

"Yeah. You look much better. Guess you just needed some fresh air."

"I guess so," she agreed.

Just then Nicole drove up and parked the car in the driveway. As she got out, she looked over at David and smiled. "Hi," she said.

"This is David Stevenson," Mollie said. "David, this is my sister Nicole."

"Hi," he said.

"We were just talking about how tough it is to start in a new school where you don't know anybody. His family just moved here from Colorado."

"But the people are really friendly," he added, and smiled at Mollie. Nicole caught the look in his eye, but Mollie didn't seem to notice. "Well, I gotta get going. See you tomorrow."

"Yeah, 'bye." Mollie followed Nicole into the house.

Mollie and Nicole came into the kitchen together. Cindy was already home, sitting at the table reading the mail. She looked up. "He's cute. Where did you meet him?"

"David? Did you see him?" Mollie said, sounding surprised. "I met him in art. You really think he's cute?"

"I saw you guys from the window. As a matter of fact, when I went looking for you the other day, I thought he might be the boy you were interested in. I figured you'd finally gotten lucky."

"I think I better forget about Tyson," Mollie sighed, putting her books down. "All I am to him is some kid that follows along after him and watches him work. I tried to develop an interest in all the things he likes. I've even changed my taste in music, but nothing seems to work."

"How about a little competition?" Nicole piped up.

"What?"

"Well, David seems insterested in you. Why not pay a little attention to him and see if it makes a difference in the way Tyson treats you?"

"That would be a rotten thing to do." Cindy jumped up. "You don't get boys through stupid tricks."

"Who says it has to be a trick? David needs a friend, and Mollie just needs to be friendly. Maybe Tyson will notice her then." Nicole paused. "On the other hand, maybe Mollie will discover something else." She winked at Cindy.

Mollie, unaware of Nicole's meaning, watched her sisters leave the room. She guessed David was kind of cute. She hadn't really looked at him closely. Could she help it if they became friends and Tyson got jealous?

Chapter Twelve

Cindy was pulling the tray of hot brownies from the oven when Mollie and Nicole came back from shopping. "Thought you went surfing this afternoon," Nicole said.

"I did, but the waves weren't that good."

"They looked pretty good to me," Nicole said. Cindy shrugged.

"This wouldn't have anything to do with Grant, would it?"

Actually it did. Cindy had had one good ride on her board before Grant showed up. She immediately decided to leave. Not that he said anything rude to her. In fact, he didn't say anything at all. But she made up some flimsy excuse to her friends and left before Karie showed up also. When she thought about it on the way home, she got angry with herself. After all, they had been her friends long before Grant had come into the picture. Now she was letting him push her away from the people she liked best.

"Cindy, you've got to stop avoiding Grant. You're making yourself miserable ," Nicole lectured.

Cindy pushed the hot pan of brownies back away from the edge of the counter, burning her fingers. "Ow," she said, putting them to her mouth. "Now look what you made me do. Go away. Can't you find someone else to bother?"

"I probably could, but if I did, you'd just sit around and feel worse."

"What am I doing?"

"Look at yourself! Since when have you preferred cooking to surfing?"

"Since I got a craving for brownies."

"Well, I think you need to get out and meet somebody new."

Cindy rolled her eyes.

"Then make up with Grant. This whole thing has gone on too long."

Scooping up Smokey, who had been rubbing against her leg and meowing angrily, Cindy started to go upstairs. "Wait a minute. Aren't you going to say anything?" Nicole called after her.

"No."

"Look, I have an idea. What are you doing tonight?"

"Gorging myself on brownies."

"How about going out with Scott and me?"

"That would be lots of fun." Cindy stopped on the stairs and the cat meowed.

"No. I mean I'll call Scott and see if one of his friends wants to go out tonight. We can double. How about it?"

Cindy looked back at her sister. "No, thanks, Nicole. I don't need you to fix me up. If I want to date, I'll date. Right now I don't want any more problems."

"Come on, Cindy," Mollie chimed in. "Maybe if you go out with other boys, Grant will notice." She started cutting the brownies.

"I don't *care* if Grant notices me anymore. We're history. Leave those brownies alone. They're mine."

Mollie put down the knife. "Well, even if you don't want to date him again, think about how it looks. He stops seeing you and right away he's hooked up with Karie, while you sit around and mope every weekend like some nerd."

"Exactly," Nicole said. "And even if you don't want to go out with Grant, what's everybody going to think if they never see you with anyone else?"

"Who cares what they think?"

"Cindy, why are you being so stubborn? No one's expecting you to develop a long-lasting relationship. Just go out with someone, for Pete's sake."

"Okay, okay. If Scott has a friend, I'll go out with him. But don't expect me to be charming," she warned.

"I'd never dream of it," Nicole said. As soon as

Cindy was out of sight, she rushed to the phone and called Scott.

"Hi, Scott. Listen, I have a favor to ask."

"Sure," he said.

"You don't happen to have any available friends that might be interested in taking Cindy out, do you?"

"I don't know. Justin might not have any plans, and he thinks your sister is kind of cute."

"Cindy?"

"Yeah, Cindy's the blond one that does all the surfing?"

"Yes."

"If he hasn't got plans, I know he'd want to go."

"That would be great. And Scott, maybe we'd better not play miniature golf tonight. Could we go to a movie instead?"

"Sure. Why?"

"Well, Cindy has this competitive spirit, and I'd just as soon keep her away from anything where she'll get the urge to show up her date. Especially the first time he meets her."

Scott laughed. "Don't worry. Justin can take care of himself."

"Don't be too sure. You've never seen Cindy in action."

Cindy was trying to shovel out the mess in the bottom of the closet when Nicole came up to tell her that Scott's friend Justin was really excited about going out with her.

"I'll bet he is," Cindy said, emerging from the closet with a tennis racket.

"No, really. He thinks you're cute."

"Uh-huh."

"He does. We're going to the movies."

"Okay."

Nicole looked at Cindy's faded sweats and disheveled hair. "And wear something—""she went to the closet and slid hangers back and forth "—else."

"I planned to," Cindy said. But when Nicole left, Cindy stood looking at the clothes in her closet. What else could she wear? She hated this. Why had she let her sisters talk her into something so stupid as a date in the first place? She didn't need to go out with anybody. She didn't have anything to prove.

Oh, well, she decided, she really had only one thing to wear. Cindy pulled her jeans skirt from the closet. She tried on several different blouses with it but wasn't happy with any of them.

Mollie was standing in the doorway when she threw off the latest flop. "My red sweater would look great with that."

"It won't fit."

"Sure it will. It's oversized. It'll look great. Here. I'll go get it."

Mollie disappeared and was back in a minute with the red sweater. She went to the closet and pulled a flannel shirt from the hanger. "Here. Try this on with it."

Cindy put on the clothes and looked at herself in the mirror. She had to admit, it looked better than anything else she'd tried on. In fact, red was a good color for her. It seemed to set off her blond hair and give her face more color.

"That looks terrific," Nicole commented, coming into the room.

"Doesn't it?" Mollie agreed.

"What do you think, Cindy?" Nicole asked as she circled her sister.

"It's okay, I guess."

"You guess?"

"Oh, I don't know. It's just that I feel so funny about all this. What if this guy doesn't really want to go at all, and he's just doing Scott a favor?"

"I told you, he knows who you are, and he really wants to go out with you. Stop worrying."

"Fine. I will. Just leave me alone." Cindy plopped down on her bed and buried her face in Smokey's warm body.

But Cindy continued to worry. All through the rest of the afternoon. All through dinner. All through getting ready to go. She worried that he might not like her. She worried even more that she might not like him. She didn't even know him. All she knew was that he was the catcher on the varsity baseball team. Maybe they could talk about baseball. She was a pretty good left fielder herself. But Nicole probably wouldn't allow any sports talk.

Cindy was dressed when she heard the doorbell. Still she sat on her bed and avoided going downstairs. "Come on," Nicole urged. "What are you waiting for?"

When Scott saw Nicole coming downstairs, he came over and put his arm about her. He led her back to Justin, and Cindy followed. "Cindy, this is Justin Bartlett. Justin, Cindy."

"Hi, she said, and for some crazy reason felt herself blushing. At least Mollie and her parents had the good sense to stay in the family room and let her die of embarrassment without an audience to witness the whole thing.

They went out to the car, and Scott opened the door for her. She climbed into the backseat and cursed both her jeans skirt and two-door cars. It felt as if Justin gave her a slight push on the rear just as she climbed in, but she thought she must be mistaken.

Before the previews began, Justin asked if she'd heard anything about the movie. She had, and she told him it was supposed to be really good. Justin agreed. "It's good to finally see a movie that tells it like it is."

"What?" Cindy asked.

"Well, they make all these dumb movies nowadays with these superhuman women in them who go around doing everything perfect and show these dumb guys who have to be saved by them, and I'm just glad to see a movie that's a little more realistic."

"Realistic," Cindy repeated. She felt herself getting angry.

"Well, you know, some stupid girl gets herself in trouble, and it's up to the guy to stick his neck out and save her butt."

"Oh, yeah?" Cindy said. That was when Nicole nudged her and suggested they go get something to drink.

"I can't believe that creep." Cindy fumed.

"Come on, Cindy. Hang in there. Just for tonight. He's a friend of Scott's. Please, don't ruin everything."

"Okay, I'll try. But I won't listen to him put women down all night. So you'd better tell Scott to tell his friend to keep his mouth shut."

When they got back to their seats, the movie was starting. Cindy sat down and told herself she would ignore Justin and enjoy the show. But it was pretty hard to ignore someone whose voice carried and who insisted on whispering rather loudly right into her ear. Every time the woman would do anything he thought was dumb, he'd point it out.

When the movie ended, Cindy went into the bathroom to splash cool water on her face and, hopefully, cool down. Nicole followed her.

"Did you like the movie?" Nicole asked.

"I don't know. I'll have to see it again when I'm not with motor mouth. It seems to be a problem with some people."

"He talked a lot, huh?"

"Oh, it wasn't just the talking, I could handle that. It was the things he was talking about." She jerked some paper towels from the machine, wiped her hands, and rammed the towels into the wastebasket.

"Well, let's go get some pizza and talk about something else."

"I don't know how much longer I can stand to be around that jerk."

"Come on," Nicole pleaded. "It won't be that bad. We'll try to keep things light, okay?"

"Okay," Cindy agreed.

Nicole stopped at the door and turned to Cindy. "Thanks. I know this hasn't been exactly what you had in mind. I appreciate your keeping things under control."

"Let's just go and get this over with before I lose it all."

Pete's was fairly deserted for a Saturday night. After they found a table, Justin asked what she wanted to drink.

"Seven Up."

"How about a Coke? Do you drink Coke? We would get a pitcher if you don't care."

"Coke is fine."

"Will a large pizza be enough?" he asked Scott. "I can eat half a pizza myself, and you probably can, too. Course the girls won't eat much." He winked at Cindy, who grimaced and turned away. Obviously, he'd never seen her eat a pizza.

He stepped to the counter and ordered for all of them. He never even asked what kind of topping they wanted. Turning to Cindy, he said, "Why don't you go on and save us a table. We'll get the drinks. Oh, and be sure to get some napkins, too, huh?"

"Why don't you see if they have a damp cloth, and we can wash the table and chairs while we wait for you?" Cindy said sarcastically.

"Hey, that's a good idea." Justin didn't notice that she wasn't serious. "You know one time we came here and I sat right in some tomato sauce."

Cindy opened her mouth to tell him what he could do, and Nicole grabbed her arm. "I think napkins will be fine."

"I can't take this much longer," she muttered under her breath.

"Only a little while. Maybe another half hour. Then you never have to talk to him again, okay?"

Cindy looked at her sister and said nothing. A half hour might not seem long to her, but another half hour with this guy would be enough to finish her off.

Cindy had never seen anyone eat so fast. He almost inhaled the pizza. One minute there was almost a whole pepperoni pizza, then in the next, there was only one piece left. He looked over at Cindy and Nicole and asked, "You girls mind if I have this last piece? Wouldn't want it to go to waste."

"By all means," Cindy said. She didn't have an appetite anyway.

She looked at the clock above the counter. It had been twenty minutes. If Nicole's estimate was right, the worst night of her life would be over in ten more minutes.

Justin leaned back and belched loudly. He grinned and said, "Excuse me." He took his hands and put them on either side of his stomach. "Ah, that was good."

"Yes, you have to keep your strength up." Cindy smiled sweetly.

"You aren't kidding. Baseball is just around the corner."

Cindy tried to steer the conversation onto safer ground. "I know. I'm on the softball team."

"You are?" Justin looked surprised. "I didn't know girls still played in high school. I mean, I remember the year I was thirteen and played summer baseball. We had this girl who wanted to play on the team." He started laughing as if it was some great joke, but Cindy stared him down. "Course she was pretty good for a girl, but you know, she couldn't really keep up, could she?"

"That's funny," Cindy said. Nicole held her breath and waited for what was coming next. "After all, most boys are so clumsy at that age. She probably had the best coordination on the team."

Justin's mouth dropped open. "Are you kidding? Girls don't have near the strength boys do at that age. Well, at any age, really. When it came time to hit the ball, she could never put a bat to it with any real power."

"I've known some fairly strong girls," Cindy said. "I've swum with some very good athletes."

"Well, swimming, sure. But that's not really a male sport. You know, not really competitive."

"What?"

"Yeah. It doesn't take much guts to get into a swimming pool. Nothing's going to happen to you. All you can get is wet." He laughed.

"Let's just see how tough you really are," Cindy said. "Put your money where your mouth is." She took out five dollars from her pocket and threw it on the table.

"What's this for?"

"Five bucks says I can beat you in arm wrestling. Right here."

"That wouldn't be fair."

"Let me worry about what's fair. Are you on or not?" Cindy had beaten a few guys before, but she was angry enough to think she could take him. She hoped his overconfidence would be his downfall.

He took five dollars out of his pocket. "You're on."

"Cindy, come on, not here." Nicole tried to put the money back.

Cindy got up and centered her chair and pushed up the sleeve of Mollie's sweater. Justin lined his chair up across from her. They clasped hands in the center of the table, and Scott started them off, while Nicole held her head in her hands.

Cindy concentrated all of her strength on keeping her arm upright. She expected the burst of power at the beginning, but she began to worry when she couldn't budge his arm. Maybe this hadn't been such a good idea. She was feeling herself slipping. She pulled her arm upright again and willed herself not to let her hand go down.

Someone sat down at the table next to them, and Justin looked up to see who it was. Cindy took that moment to make a move and forced his hand toward the table. Cindy saw the pitcher fly off the table and crash to the floor. She heard a scream and looked over at the booth across from them.

Coke was everywhere and spreading rapidly across the floor. She looked at the table and saw Grant and Karie. Karie jumped to her feet, and Cindy saw the dark stains all over her light-colored pants. Grant grabbed a handful of napkins and helped her blot her shoes and slacks.

"Sorry," Cindy said.

"Do me a favor," Grant said tersely. "Next time you're going to be out in public, give me a call so I can stay out of your way!"

Chapter Thirteen

Monday afternoon Mollie came in from school after an art meeting, carrying a large object. She tried to set it on the table in the kitchen, but it kept falling over. At least Mollie told Cindy it was falling over. The thing was so grossly misshapen that it was hard to tell which was the right side up.

"Know what that is?" she asked.

"I give up." Cindy looked up from her sandwich.

"No, really, what is it?"

"You tell me." Cindy got up and took a closer look at it. It looked like a glob of clay to her. But she assumed Mollie meant it to be something more. She picked it up. There were three things sticking out of it that were all different sizes and lengths and a sort of blob on the top of that.

Cindy held it up to eye level and carefully evaluated it.

"Is it a stool like they use for milking cows?" she asked, having the feeling it most probably wasn't.

"No. Look," Mollie said, pointing to a round lump on the top. Or at least what Cindy thought might be the top. "Guess again."

Cindy handed it back to Mollie and said, "Hmm. I'm not into art. You'd better tell me."

"It's Winston!" she said.

"Winston?"

"Well, actually, it was *supposed* to be Winston," she said skeptically as she reexamined the work.

"Last time I looked, Winston had four legs. And they were all the same size."

"Well, he did have four legs, but one of them fell off in the kiln, and the clay sort of shrunk up at different stages, so they're not the same size anymore."

Cindy looked at the three stumps on the bottom. "Oh, well, that explains it," she said. "Mollie, stick to flirting. If Tyson gets a look at this thing, you don't have a chance."

"Thanks a lot. If you're going to be sarcastic, I just won't show you any more of my work." She cradled the sculpture in her hands. "Great artists aren't made overnight," she reminded her sister.

But Cindy had already left the room. At the top of the stairs, she saw Winston lying outside Nicole's door. She kneeled down beside him and said, "I was right; you *do* have four legs." He got to his feet, wagging his tail. Cindy petted his head then got up and went to her room. She picked up her mathbook and sat at her desk.

She was suddenly jolted from the chair by a loud blast of symphonic music. "Mollie!" she shouted. "Turn that thing down. I'm trying to study."

Mollie didn't respond, and the music continued to blare. Cindy got up and went to Mollie's room. She marched over to the stereo and turned the volume down.

"What do you think you're doing?" Mollie asked, climbing out from inside her closet.

"My homework. And I can't concentrate with that noise shattering my eardrums."

"Cindy, you don't have any taste."

"Neither do you. You just don't have enough sense to know it." She went back to her own room, leaving Mollie to contemplate her meaning.

The following day, Mollie saw David sitting in the ceramic room when she came down to the art room after school. He was glazing a pot he'd thrown earlier.

"That's nice," she said, leaning on the table to get a better look at it.

"You ready for a lesson yet?" he asked her.

"I don't know. If I can't even sculpt, you think I can really learn to do that?" She pointed to the beautiful piece of pottery in front of him.

"It's easy. Really. The wheel does all the work. Come on, I'll show you."

She went to the potter's wheel and sat on the stool across from him.

"To start with, you need to wedge the clay like this." He tossed the clay onto the wheel several times. "This takes the air bubbles out of it. Then ball it up and put it in the center of the wheel like this."

He reached down and turned the wheel on. He dipped his hands into the water and soaked the clay. "Now you have to center the clay," he told her. He pressed the clay flat and pulled it into a peak.

"That doesn't look much like a pot to me," she said.

"It will. Give it time. Right now I'm still centering it."

He put his thumb into the center of the pot and began to pull the sides out. The clay was only a few inches high. Mollie watched in amazement as he used his two fingers to pull the pot into shape.

"You use this thing," he said, showing her a tool in his hand. "It's a rib tool, and it will shape the pot for you. Then this chamois will give you a lip." He stopped talking to finish the pot on the wheel. He turned it off and took a wire tool from the table next to him.

"Now you cut it from the wheel, and you're ready to fire it."

"You make it look so easy."

"It is. Here. Sit down."

She took an apron from the pegs on the wall and straddled the wheel. Lifting the lump of clay, she threw it against the wheel as he'd done.

"Throw it a little harder. It doesn't bruise or anything."

She got it centered, and he turned the wheel on. "Now get your hands wet and put the water on the clay," he instructed.

"Remember to keep your elbows in."

She pulled them back. As the wheel spun in front of her, she was trying to remember what he had done next. It had looked so easy when David did it.

He talked her through it, and when he turned the wheel off, she looked at her slightly lopsided pot and said, "I don't think this is going to be any better than my sculpting."

He smiled at her and said, "It just takes time."

"Maybe I'll be the person who collects art instead of the one who creates it."

"Come on," he said, smashing her pot back into a ball. "Try it again."

She decided that it was definitely a better effort than her portrayal of Winston. So she did. She tried it several more times that day, and by Thursday she was able to get the pot to stay the same size on all sides. She was finally getting the hang of "pulling the walls up from the floor," as David called it.

Thursday afternoon she sat in front of her latest effort and felt more than a little proud of herself. "Hey, that looks pretty good," David said.

"You think so?"

"Looks like the student could outdo the teacher one of these days."

"You really think it's good?"

"It's good," he reassured her. Mollie noticed that he had friendly brown eyes and a strong chin.

"I'll say it is," Tyson said, coming into the pottery room and hanging up his apron. "Did you do this?"

"Yes," Mollie said, feeling herself blush with pride.

"You've been wasting your time with sculpture. You've got a talent for pottery."

"I don't know about that. I just had a good teacher."

"You've been a pretty good student," David interrupted.

"Thanks, David."

Tyson sat down next to her and began talking about the possibility of her entering one of her pots in the art show.

"Gee, I don't know. Why not use some of David's work. He's much better than I am."

"Well, we'll use his work, too. But the more we have to submit, the better showing we'll have. Don't you think, Dave?"

"Hmmm? Oh, yeah. Look, I've got to get going.

I'll see you guys later." David got up and left in a rush.

Mollie watched him go with mixed feelings. Here she was sitting alone with Tyson, which was what she had been hoping for for weeks, and now she wanted to go after David. After all, he was the one who had helped her and taken the time to teach her. It didn't seem right that she should be sharing the glory with Tyson. He'd never even noticed what she was doing.

All of a sudden she got up, pulled her apron over her head, and hung it on the peg. "I've got to go, too," she said.

"What's your hurry? I can give you a ride home."

"That's okay. Thanks anyway. I'll see you later," Mollie called over her shoulder.

She rushed out the front of the building and looked down the street. She didn't see David anywhere. Darn! She wanted to catch him before he got very far so it would look like she'd just happened to catch up with him.

"Looking for someone?" David asked, coming up behind her.

"Well, um . . . you, I guess."

"I had to stop by my locker, and I went back to the art room to see if you were ready to go, and Tyson said you'd already left. Come on, I'll walk you home."

Mollie looked at David's blond hair in the late-afternoon sun. It had a warm golden tint to it. Every once in a while when he was excited or nervous, he'd reach up and run his hand through it, and it would fall softly back in place. Funny, she'd never really noticed how cute he was before. He laughed a lot, too. And when he smiled, his dimples would crease his cheeks. It was so easy to be with him.

Mollie began to realize she hadn't really thought about Tyson in a long time. At first she thought it was because she had been engrossed in her pottery. Then she realized it was because she was thinking about David these days.

"So what happened to the big talk with Tyson?"

"Nothing. I just had to get going."

"I thought the ultimate high would be a chance for the two of you to be alone in the pottery room."

"Why would you think that?"

"Come on, Mollie, I'm not blind. I've seen the way you looked at him. Do you think anyone with your knack for sculpture hangs around an art room for weeks trying to learn something they aren't much good at and don't much like to do just because they want to broaden their horizons?"

"It was that obvious, huh?"

"Yeah. So what happened? He said he offered you a ride home and you didn't take it."

"Guess I felt like walking." She smiled. "I need the exercise."

"Umm. Well . . . do you have plans for tomorrow night?" he asked suddenly.

"No."

"Want to make some?"

"Sure."

"Mollie, you're entirely too young to be going on a date," her mother said firmly.

"But Mom, he's really nice. He just moved here."

"If he just moved here, you can't know that much about him."

Cindy opened the back door and said, "What's all the commotion about?"

"Mollie wants to go out Friday night with some boy, and she's not old enough to be dating yet."

"Who's the lucky guy?" Cindy asked. "Tyson?"

"No, David."

"David," Cindy said, raising her eyebrows in approval. "He's nice, Mom. Let her go."

"Nice is not a qualification for taking my fourteen-year-old daughter on a date."

"Come on, Mom, lighten up. Mollie can take care of herself," Cindy said, then leaned over and said in a loud whisper, "Relax. If she won't let you go out with him, tell her you're going to the movies with a friend and meet him there." She winked and left the room.

"Cindy Lewis. I heard that. You come back here."

Mollie widened her eyes and looked at her mother. "You don't want me to be forced to lie to you, do you, Mom?"

* * *

Mollie's father put another helping of green beans on his plate. "Your mother tells me you want to go out on a date this weekend, Mollie."

"Dad, he's real nice. I bet if you met him you'd really like him."

"Where did *you* meet him?"

"In the art club. He's a great artist, and he taught me to use the potter's wheel and everything."

"Sounds like the basis for a solid romance to me."

"This is no joking matter," her mother reminded him.

"How old is he?" he asked.

"Fifteen. He's a sophomore."

"So he can't drive. That's good. How well do you know him?"

"I've seen him practically every day for the last two weeks, and he hasn't attacked me yet."

"Well, if he drops by here first and we get a chance to meet him, I suppose it will be all right."

"Oh, thank you, Daddy," Mollie said, jumping up and throwing her arms around her father's neck.

"Just the same, I want you home by ten-thirty, or this may be the last date you have until your twenty-first birthday."

"I promise," she said. Mollie's heart was racing so much she could hardly finish eating.

* * *

The next day David picked her up at six and his dad drove them to the mall. He dropped them off and said he'd be back to get them at nine. They went into the mall and had fun going into all the shops and trying on outrageous clothes. They stopped for dinner at one of the Mexican restaurants. Mollie burned her mouth on the hot sauce, and David said, "You Californians don't know what hot really is. Come to Colorado sometime and eat Mexican food."

"Mexican food? In Colorado?"

"Of course."

"I thought they'd just have regular food there."

"Mexican food is regular food. It's just Mexican." They ate off each other's plates, and David decided he liked her food better than he liked his, and Mollie decided she liked his food better than hers. So they traded.

Nine o'clock came much too soon for Mollie. She never thought she could have so much fun. "I'll walk home from here," David told his father when they were a few blocks from Mollie's house.

He took Mollie's hand. "What time do you have to be home?"

"Ten-thirty," she said with a shrug of apology.

"Let's walk down to the beach."

The water rolled gently in, and the moon cast an eerie light on the waves. Mollie led him to her favorite spot, where they sat down to watch the water.

"Bet you don't have anything like this in Colorado."

"No, but we do have the Rockies. They can be just as beautiful," he said with a touch of homesickness. Then he looked at Mollie. "But we don't have anyone like you."

He leaned over and kissed her on the cheek. "You make the whole move worthwhile."

"Really?" she said, smiling up at him.

"Honest." It was like a dream come true. Who would have thought that all the while she was daydreaming about falling in love, it would have been someone who just walked into her life? She hadn't even picked him out. Maybe that was what love was all about.

He got up and held his hand out to her. They began walking down the beach. "David, have you dated lots of other girls?"

"Not really."

"I must seem pretty inexperienced to you," she said.

"No, you seem pretty perfect."

Mollie decided if ever there was a time in her life when she felt almost perfect, it was tonight.

Chapter Fourteen

The week had gone by rather slowly. Cindy wasn't sure whether it was because she'd stayed home the weekend before or because her teachers had piled on a lot of homework or because she was missing Grant. By Wednesday she decided it was the latter.

She was late getting out of sixth period because she had stayed to ask some questions about a government paper, so the halls were fairly deserted when she finally got to her locker. She was trying to stuff the junk back into it and slam it closed before everything came cascading out again, when someone came up behind her.

"Looks like a two-man job to me."

Cindy spun around and saw Grant smiling down at her. He held her books in place while she set the rest of the things in on top of them. "Thanks," she said.

"No problem."

She turned to rearrange her books that were sliding from her grasp.

"So how have you been?" he asked.

"Fine."

"I haven't seen you around much."

"Not since the other night at Pete's, I guess," she said, looking down and trying not to smile.

"Yeah, not since then."

"How have you been?"

"Good." They were walking toward the doors that led out to the parking lot. "You done much surfing lately?" he asked.

"No. It's been pretty cold," she said.

"Yeah. I haven't been out much either."

"There you are." Grant and Cindy looked up and saw Karie coming toward them. She was dressed in her cheerleading outfit. "We finished practice early." She looked at Cindy in an odd way and said, "Hi, Cindy." She turned back to Grant without giving her a chance to say anything. "How about giving me a ride home?"

"Well, sure," he said. He looked at Cindy. "Want a ride?"

"No, that's okay. I've got my bike." She smiled briefly at the two of them. "See you around."

"Yeah, see ya," Grant said.

Karie smiled sweetly at Cindy and looped her arm possessively through Grant's as she led him down the hall toward her locker. Cindy looked at them just once before she left the building. She could have sworn Grant was looking back at her, too. Maybe it was just wishful thinking.

She was crossing the parking lot toward the bike rack, and a car pulled up beside her and honked. Taylor rolled down the window and yelled, "Hey, want a ride? We can put it on the rack."

She hesitated. What if Grant saw her getting in his car after she'd turned him down? But it was late, and suddenly she just wanted to get home.

"Okay," she said as they put her bike on the rack. "How come you're still here so late?"

"Actually, I've been home once already, but I forgot something for my term paper. If I get this term paper written and live to tell about it, it'll be a miracle."

"I know." Cindy nodded. "We haven't started them yet. I'm not looking forward to it. I've never had to do footnotes before, and I don't know how to make a bibliography. I'm just glad I don't have to work on this and my government report at the same time. I'd never get out of the library."

"Speaking of the library," he said, "I've got to go over there tonight. If you have to work on something, I could give you a ride."

"Okay." That seemed like a good thing to do. Taylor was nice enough, and she *did* have to get this dumb report finished this week. If she failed government, she would be ineligible for the swim team, and the coach would kill her.

"I'll pick you up at about seven o'clock," he said, stopping in front of her house.

Cindy was copying some information from one of the resource books and looked over at Taylor. He was watching her again. She looked away, but she could sense he was still looking at her. She closed the book and got up.

"You're never going to get that report written if all you do is watch me work." She went to the front desk and traded her book for another reserve text. She came back to the table.

"Can I help it if you hold my attention a lot better than Ralph Waldo Emerson?"

Cindy smiled. She wished that all of her competition were about as interesting as Emerson and about as much alive. She thought about Karie Simmons.

"I think I know what might help me keep my mind on this," he said, doodling on the pad in front of him. "Tell me you'll go out with me Friday night, and I can concentrate on my homework. See, I've been sitting here trying to think of ways to get up the nerve to ask you out, and I can't think of anything."

Cindy laughed. "I'd say you just did."

The librarian *shhh*ed them, and Cindy lowered her voice. "Sure, I'll go out with you." She opened her book and saw that he was still looking at her. "But you'd better get busy, or we'll spend Friday night trying to write these dumb reports."

When Cindy got home, Mollie and Nicole were excited when Cindy told them she was going out with Taylor Friday night. "It's no big deal," she said. "We're going over to the arcade. Just play a few video games, maybe some miniature golf. He's just a friend."

Cindy saw Nicole wink at Mollie, who smiled back knowingly.

"Hey, you two, stop making this into more than it is."

Taylor was fifteen minutes early Friday, and he ended up having to wait with her parents in the family room while she finished getting dressed. Mollie came up and said, "You'd better hurry. Dad's got him on the hot seat down there. So far, we've gone through elementary school and junior high, and he's headed straight toward, 'So what are you planning to do with your life?' "

"Okay, I'm almost ready," Cindy said. She grabbed a sweater from the closet and pulled it on as she went out the door.

"Wait a minute," Nicole said, taking her by the arm. "You messed up your hair." She fluffed Cindy's hair with her fingers, and Cindy shrugged away from her.

"Stop it."

"Have fun," Mollie said as Cindy hopped down the stairs. She planned to. It had been a long time since she had been on a date with anyone special. She wasn't sure that Taylor was going to be all that special, but he sure had Justin beat already, and they hadn't even left the house.

When they got to the arcade, Cindy headed straight to the video games. "I love these," Taylor said. "Do you play them much?"

"Some," Cindy said. "I used to play them a lot more, but I still like to play them when I can."

He put a quarter in the machine. "Be my guest."

After a few minutes, Cindy had forgotten all about Taylor standing at her side. As she played, she racked up more and more men to fight the invading armies, and the total on the machine kept climbing.

"That's amazing," Taylor said. Cindy looked over at him and felt guilty that he wasn't getting to play. "You don't have to stay here," she said.

"It's okay. I like this game."

"Well, here," she said, stepping aside. "I have a cramp in my hand. Play for a while." She moved out of the way and began massaging her hand. She didn't really have a cramp, but she didn't want him to miss out on all the fun.

Cindy moved over to another machine, where some boy was doing very well. She watched him expertly maneuver the electronic blips on the screen. By the time she wandered back to Taylor, she found that several of her men had been wiped out. He handed the control back to her.

"You'd better do this before I get your armies totally annihilated."

Cindy played for a while until she finally got

bored with it. Taylor seemed to prefer watching her to playing himself.

"Want to try the bumper cars?" she asked as they left the video arcade.

"Sure."

Cindy loved the bumper cars. It was fun to smash into people. She thought for a moment how much fun it would be if she saw Karie in one of the little cars, then turned her attention back to Taylor.

Cindy got into her car first, and Taylor was surprised when she rammed the side of his. Taylor backed up and took a run at her. Cindy felt her head jerk when he crashed into her. She backed up and went after him. They crashed and laughed and threatened each other until the ride was over. They got out and were facing the entrance to the miniature golf. "Want to try?" Cindy asked.

"I have to warn you, I'm not very good. I mean, I never have gotten the hang of it. The first time I send the ball into the next green, and then I barely tap it and it hardly moves."

"You just need a lesson," she said.

They each got a putter and a different-colored ball. Taylor was right. He certainly wasn't very good at it. Cindy showed him how to hold the putter and position himself in front of the ball so he could line it up with the hole. But he kept taking his putter back as if it were a nine iron. Cindy showed him how to slide it back and glide it through the ball.

By the eighteenth hole, he had finally gotten to where he could par a hole once in a while. Cindy beat him pretty badly, and she hadn't even been trying.

Maybe it was because Taylor didn't have much of a competitive spirit. He complimented her on everything she did, though. Rather than try to outdo her, he stood back and admired how she did it. After a while, she got tired of his constant praise.

They turned in their golf clubs and got a hot dog. They found an empty table and sat down. "Boy, Cindy, you're really amazing," he said.

"Thanks," she said, though she wasn't sure just what she'd done that was so incredible.

"Is there anything you can't do?"

She laughed. "There's plenty."

"I don't know if I believe that. I've seen you swim, surf, play video games and golf. You're terrific at everything. How do you do it?"

She smiled and thought about all the things she couldn't do. Like put on a long formal and go to a dance and act charming and witty. Sure, she could impress her dates if they were looking for athletic ability, but she didn't stand a chance when it came down to being a lady.

"Do you want to go bowling tomorrow?" he asked.

"I'm sorry. I can't. I've already got plans." Taylor was a nice guy, but it was a bit like going on a date with someone's younger brother. He had *ooh*ed and *aah*ed over everything she did. He didn't really encourage her to try her best, and he was just too easy to impress. If she kept going out with him, she would quit pushing herself. She was used to boys like Grant and Duffy, who made her work for her accomplishments. Taylor was, well, rather boring and just too nice.

She looked over at Taylor and saw him staring at her with that goofy smile on his face. Suddenly Cindy was very anxious to get home.

Cindy lay on her bed in the dark bedroom and wondered why she had been such a dope. She had had the perfect relationship with Grant, and all she had wanted was to break free of him. Now that she looked back on it, she realized she had been the one who had felt stifled and committed. He had never said anything about not wanting to go places with her.

She had been the one who had tried to leave him behind. Well, she'd left him behind all right, but she hadn't gone any further than she'd been weeks ago. In fact, she felt as if she would have to run to catch up to the person she'd been.

The world was full of guys, but very few of them were like Grant. She thought about the warm feeling she'd gotten just when he came up behind her at her locker the other day and helped her with her books. And the sinking feeling she'd had when she saw him walk away with Karie.

Had she been foolish enough to give up the one

perfect relationship just to be saddled with boys like Justin, who thought girls were empty-headed and weak, or Taylor, who thought everything she did was perfect?

She needed an honest relationship—like the one she'd had with Grant. He had let her be the person she was, but she hadn't given him the same consideration. She thought about all the advice and arguments Nicole and Mollie had given her and she hadn't listened to when she was fighting against the pull Grant had on her. She would give anything to feel that tug again.

"Cindy Lewis, you're a fool," she whispered in the darkness. "Sometimes you ought to listen to someone besides yourself."

Chapter Fifteen

The next morning Cindy went for her usual run to the beach, hoping it would make her feel better. But it didn't work. Coming into the house, she heard the phone ringing. "Anybody home?" she called. There was no answer, and she rushed to answer the phone before whoever it was hung up.

"Cindy? It's me. Duffy. I was about to give up on you."

"Hi, Duffy. What's going on?"

"Not much. The weather's so nice today, I thought maybe you'd help me get a beach party organized."

"Great." She really needed the company today. "What do you want me to do?"

"Well, a bunch of people are bringing hot dogs and buns. How about bringing some drinks? We'll put it all together when we get here and hope there's enough for all of us. Tell Nicole and Mollie to come, too," he said.

He hesitated, and Cindy thought he was getting ready to hang up. She was just about to tell him good-bye when she heard him say, "You can bring a date."

"Who would I bring, Duffy?"

"I don't know. Who do you like these days?"

They both knew the answer to that.

"I think I'll just bring my surfboard."

"Cindy, there's something else you should know."

"Yeah?"

"Well, Grant's going to be there, and he's probably going to have Karie with him. I almost didn't tell you, because I really want you to come. But I didn't want you to get all upset when you saw them there together."

"Don't be silly, Duffy. Why would I get upset?"

"I've noticed how you sort of fade out of the picture whenever he's around, and I don't like it. Cindy, you're my friend, too, and I don't want you to stop hanging out with us just because Grant's around. And, well, we all like Grant, too. I just wish he would stop being so stubborn and admit he still likes you."

"Sure, he does. How much can he like me when he hasn't been without Karie since we broke up?"

"I still talk to him sometimes, Cindy. I know what he's thinking." Then he said, "It wouldn't hurt if you asked someone to the beach, though.

It might do him good to see someone else paying attention to you."

"Thanks, I'll keep that in mind."

Cindy hung up and wondered who she could possibly ask. Most of the boys she would have wanted to ask were just good friends, and they would be there already. Of course, they'd probably have dates.

Cindy thought about calling Taylor and then imagined what a day at the beach would be like with him. If she did take a ride on her surfboard, he would probably be waiting at the shore, jumping up and down like a cheerleader, telling her how wonderful she was. Maybe that was what Karie did for Grant. She pictured the two of them standing next to each other and waiting for Cindy and Grant to come back. But maybe they would just peddle out in the water and wait for the sun to set and never come back for days.

"Whatever you're thinking, it must be good," her mother said, coming in the back door.

"What?" Cindy said, jumping up.

"Well, from the smile on your face, you've either gotten that government paper back and you did extremely well, or you've got a date with someone special."

"Neither one, Mom. I'm just thinking." She took her book bag off the table and grabbed an apple. "I'll be up in my room."

Mollie was all excited when Cindy told her about the cookout. She called David right away.

"Oh, David, you'll love it," Cindy heard her say. "It's what living in California is all about. You won't miss Colorado for a minute once you've been to a real beach party."

Cindy closed the door to her room and shut out her little sister's voice. All of a sudden Cindy wasn't that elated about the party. She probably would have been if she hadn't known that Grant would be showing up with Karie.

She didn't stand a chance with Karie around. Whenever Karie appeared, Grant gave her all of his attention. She'd just have to get used to it, Cindy told herself. It looked as if she had lost Grant for good.

Nicole knocked softly at the door. "Are you wearing a swimsuit to the beach?" she asked, sitting on Cindy's bed.

"I don't know. I guess so. Maybe I'll just wear shorts."

"You could borrow one of my suits."

"Come on, Nicole. You don't own a suit that isn't a tiny two-piece. I can't surf in that."

"Why not forget surfing for a day and concentrate on getting a certain person to notice you again?"

"Who? Grant?"

Nicole nodded.

"Look, Nicole, he noticed me the first time, and I wasn't wearing a two-piece. He'll notice me again if he really wants to."

"Well, if you change your mind, the offer still

stands." She got up and said, "I'm going to make some fresh lemonade for the party."

"Great," Cindy said. "Why don't you make some sandwiches, too?"

A few hours later, Cindy stood in front of her mirror and looked at her blue shorts and baggy faded T-shirt. She needed to do something with her hair, too. It was too long in all the wrong places. Maybe she needed a new hairstyle. She pulled the hair back of her already short hair up behind her head to see how it would look if she went really short with it.

"Is that what you're wearing?" Mollie asked critically from the doorway. She had on purple floral print jams over her swimsuit and a sleeveless sweatshirt top.

Nicole stopped by and leaned on the door. She had on a pink sundress, and her silky brown hair was tied back in a french braid, woven with a matching ribbon. Cindy looked back at her reflection in the mirror and then at her sisters and was even more unhappy with what she saw. Everyone else would be dressed like her sisters, and she'd show up looking like one of the guys.

"I don't know about you," Nicole told Mollie, "but I think Cindy needs some first aid."

She pulled out the chair and forcefully pushed Cindy into it. "Hey, what are you doing?"

"Making you worth noticing."

Cindy didn't say anything.

Mollie went into her room and looked for something more stylish to lend Cindy. She came back shaking her head. "Everything's dirty. Better try your closet," she told Nicole.

"Here, do this," Nicole instructed.

Mollie took the styling gel and spritzed it on Cindy's hair. She combed back the sides and fluffed up the top. Then she took up some mascara.

"Wait a minute," Cindy said, pushing her hand back. "That junk will come off in the water and run all over my face."

"No, it won't. It's waterproof, and I'm just barely putting it on."

"Then why bother?"

"Cindy, stop being difficult," Nicole told her sternly as she returned with a pair of yellow shorts and an orange-and-white top. She handed Cindy one of her two-piece suits to wear under it.

"I can't fill this thing out," Cindy complained.

"You'd be surprised," Nicole told her.

Once Cindy was dressed, Nicole asked, "Now what do you think?"

Cindy looked in the mirror, and she had to admit it was an improvement. "Okay, okay," she grumbled. "Let's get going."

They went through the kitchen and loaded up the food and drinks into an ice chest. Cindy felt her appetite coming back. She had a feeling that this might just turn out to be a good day after all.

Chapter Sixteen

The Lewis girls were among the first to arrive. Duffy and Anna were setting up portable barbecues and claiming a section of the beach for everyone. With the sudden change of weather, the place would fill up quickly with Californians ready to face the sun again.

Kids dribbled in all afternoon. Cindy got warm toward midday and took off her top. She noticed Duffy staring at her a couple of times and felt self-conscious. She pulled her arms around her. "Don't do that," Anna said. "You look good." Duffy nodded in agreement.

Cindy felt herself turning red, and it wasn't from the sun. That was the first time Duffy had ever looked at her like that. After a while, though, she was so busy setting up the barbecue she forgot about it.

Mollie ran off as soon as David arrived. He took her hand and they walked slowly back to the rest of the group. He smiled at everyone but was still pretty shy with most people. Everyone except Mollie, Cindy noticed. Cindy watched as Mollie led him down the beach. They walked hand in hand, and Cindy envied her little sister's happiness. She also hoped that if things didn't work out for the two of them, Mollie would spring back faster than she had. Of course, it wouldn't be so hard for her. She couldn't imagine Mollie feeling low for too long. She was cute and perky and she knew how to flirt with boys.

"Well, look who's here," Cindy heard, and turned to see who the voice belonged to, though she already had a pretty good idea.

"Hello, Justin," she said evenly.

"You look terrific." He leaned down and wrapped his arms around her bare waist. Aware of his flesh against hers, she wished she had worn her dependable one-piece. She tried to stand up.

"Cindy, could you give me a hand over here?" Nicole called.

"Excuse me," Cindy said, breaking free of his grip.

"That's okay. I'll be here when you get done."

"That's what I'm afraid of," Cindy said under her breath. "Thanks," she said to Nicole.

"Looked like you needed some help. And I feel a bit responsible." She smiled at Cindy.

Cindy took the aluminum foil out of the basket, and they began covering the grill.

"What are you cooking for us?" Justin asked, coming over to sit on the blanket next to her.

"*Someone's* cooking hot dogs," Cindy said, and turned her back on him.

She was putting the foil back when Duffy called. "Cindy, come on. We're playing volleyball, and I want you on my side."

"No way," Anna protested.

"But you said you wanted to divide the teams up evenly between the girls and boys."

"Yeah, but Cindy's not like a girl."

"Thanks, Anna," Cindy said, frowning at her friend.

"I didn't mean it that way," she said, looking over at Cindy. "I meant that you can spike a ball better than any of them." She pointed to the other boys on Duffy's team.

Cindy took her place on Duffy's side and got ready to receive the serve. Jason served the ball, and she set it to Duffy, who set it back for a spike. She caught sight of Grant's red Trans Am just as she jumped. The ball went into the net.

"Maybe you can keep her after all," Jason teased. "Hey, throw the ball over here."

Cindy tossed the ball extra-hard and hoped it would knock him over. He caught it, and she got back in place for the next serve.

"Got room for two more?" Grant asked, walking up with Karie cemented to his arm, as usual. Cindy looked away down the beach.

"Sure, but you'll have to split up. We're keeping the sides even. Boys and girls."

"Okay. I'll play on this side," Grant said, stepping in next to Cindy and whipping off his shirt.

Karie stuck out her lip and said, "Maybe I'll sit this one out, Grant. I won't be much fun if they get you and the other team is stuck with me. I'm not a jock like some girls." She stared right at Cindy, who smiled at her. Grant frowned.

"Suit yourself, but do something pretty soon," Jason said. "We want to get on with this game before the sun sets."

"Come on, Karie. It's not that tough," Mike argued.

"Okay." She went to the other side and crouched down the way she saw everyone else do.

"Don't worry. I'll cover for you," Mike said over his shoulder. "Just stand back when the ball comes toward you and let me take it."

Cindy moved into place and Grant moved over beside her. "You trying to get a tan?" he asked, nodding to her bare midsection.

Before she could answer him, the ball sailed over the net and right toward them. Cindy bumped it into the air for a set, and Grant spiked it into the opposite court.

"No fair," Karie whined. "Grant's too tall. Put him in the back row."

"He'll rotate around. That's how you play," Anna said. Cindy caught the sarcasm in her voice and felt slightly sorry for Karie. She sure wasn't much of an athlete. Then she reminded herself Karie was the one who had Grant now.

It had been a great day for sun and surf. Cindy had taken several good rides on her surfboard. Grant and Duffy and the other guys had dared her to catch a big wave, and she'd wiped out. But she didn't care. Everyone fell off at some point. She just got right back on her board and rode the wave into shore. When she came off her board, Justin was waiting for her.

"You're pretty good. Here, let me get that for you." He tried to take her board, but she pulled it back.

"I can manage." She pushed it into the sand and went over to join Mollie around the campfire. The sun was starting to go down, and she felt chilly. Wrapping herself into a big beach towel, she sat down by the roaring fire. She took a marshmallow from the bag and stuck it on the end of the stick and began to roast it.

Reaching out, she pulled the crispy outside off and looked across the campfire to catch Grant watching her. He was smiling, and Karie was sitting a few feet away, pouting. She looked away and talked to Mollie. Mollie seemed to resent the intrusion, however, as she and David were deep into some conversation.

Just then Justin dropped to the sand beside her. "Nice out here, isn't it?"

She shivered. She didn't know if it was because of her wet bathing suit or a sudden chill in the air.

"Here, let me warm you up."

She started to pull away and then saw Grant with Karie beside him. She almost leaned into Justin but then decided she'd had enough game-playing.

"You could be really great if you weren't always trying to prove something," she heard Justin say.

"I don't know what you mean." She turned around and looked him directly in the eyes.

"Well, I like you well enough, Cindy, but I don't know why you get so offended when I try to help you out." She gave him a puzzled look. "You know, like when you insisted on carrying your board or wanting to open your own doors. How come you don't like anybody doing things for you?"

"I can do those things myself. Why should you do it?"

"I don't mind. It's a man's job to do those things."

Not this again, Cindy thought. "I'm going for a walk." She stood up.

"Sounds good. I'll come with you." He noticed the expression on her face and asked in what sounded like a hesitant tone, "Do you mind?"

"No," she lied. Actually she minded a lot. She wanted to be alone. No, that wasn't true. She wanted to be with Grant. But all of a sudden she felt sort of sorry for Justin. He didn't seem to know he was a creep.

She went to the rock where she sat often on her Saturday-morning jogs. She sat down and drew her legs up close to her. She felt Justin slide onto the rock beside her.

"Hmmm. It's still warm from the sun," he said. Then he leaned forward and kissed the back of her neck.

"What do you think you're doing?" she asked sharply, leaning away from him.

"Kissing you."

"I know that," Cindy said, getting to her feet. "What I want to know is why."

"Why not?"

"We don't even like each other very much. Why should we be kissing?"

"Maybe you don't like me much, but I think you're pretty cute." He got off the rock and put his arms around her. She felt him increase the pressure of his grip. This was just great. If she got into a contest of strength with him, she knew he would win.

"Let me go, Justin."

"Come on, Cindy. What's wrong with a few kisses?"

"Let me go," she said, and shoved him away.

He backed off but remained standing in front of her.

"Why don't you leave?" She turned around at Grant's voice and saw him standing a few feet away. He had put on a light green sweater over his faded jeans. He stood with his arms crossed, and a menacing expression on his face. Cindy breathed in quickly.

"What business is it of yours?"

"Never mind. Just go."

"Fine. I didn't want to be with her anyway."

"Well, I do."

Cindy looked at Grant gratefully and Justin stalked off down the beach.

"Guess I made him mad, huh?" Grant asked with a smile, his dimple deepening.

"Looks that way. Thanks. You can go back to Karie now." She was surprised to find herself talking naturally.

"Karie's gone."

"Oh? Where'd she go?" she asked, feeling her heart speed up.

"Home, I guess. We decided we weren't exactly suited for each other. Things didn't exactly work out."

"Oh."

"See, I used to date this one girl, and she was lots of fun most of the time." He moved over and sat on the rock. "We had a lot in common, and we both liked the same things. I miss her a lot, but I don't know how to tell her."

"The same thing happened to me," Cindy said, sitting down next to him.

"No kidding?" He took her hand. His felt warm.

"I thought this guy I liked wanted someone else who was different—more feminine. I had almost given up on him."

"Don't do that," he said.

"I didn't." Cindy looked at him. "I thought maybe he didn't like me anymore. I gave him plenty of reasons."

He brushed her hair gently across her forehead with his hand. "I think he still likes you." Grant leaned over and kissed her.

"You doing anything special tomorrow?" he asked, his face still close to hers.

"What do you have in mind?" She smiled.

"I thought I'd take you to some stores and pick out a couple of long dresses. If the school has another formal dance, I'd hate to miss it just because you couldn't find anything to wear."

She put her arms around him and kissed him. "I would, too. I sure missed you, Grant."

"I missed you, too." The noises of the beach party drifted across the sand, but Cindy had trouble hearing them. She'd wiped out, but she'd picked herself up and she knew she was on firm ground again.

Here's a sample of what awaits you in ON THIN ICE, book six in the "Sisters" series for GIRLS ONLY.

Cindy admired the ski instructor, though she hadn't had a chance to introduce herself yet or to strike up a real conversation. Her name was Lisa; she was from Idaho and was an alternate on the U.S. Olympic ski team. Somehow, the tall athletic young woman reminded Cindy of herself. And for the first time Cindy wished that her own favorite sport, surfing, was part of the summer Olympic regimen because suddenly she knew in her heart that she had what it took to make a national team.

"So folks," Lisa switched off the monitor and turned on the overhead lights. "I think these tapes will be helpful. Let's head out to the lifts now and hit the courses."

Cindy positioned herself right behind Lisa on the lift line. "I missed yesterday's session," Cindy said earnesly, "but I hope I can learn enough to at least get me started in ski racing."

Lisa took in Cindy's athletic physique and eager

expression and smiled. "You look like a good racer already. How long have you skied?" She asked.

"Cindy Lewis! What are you doing here?" Herb Horton's voice rang out. Everyone in the class turned his or her head and stared at the awkward figure in snowshoes clumsily making his way toward Cindy.

"Oh, boy!" Cindy grunted through her teeth. "Hi Herb," she said brusquely.

Herb shook his head woefully. "You can't take this course. You're not old enough. You have to be eighteen. . . ." his voice trailed off as he saw Cindy's livid expression.

"You're not going to listen to him, are you?" Cindy frantically grabbed Lisa's sleeve. She had totally forgotten about the age requirement for the course. "He doesn't even know me. He just follows me everywhere!" Cindy glared at Herb. But Herb appeared undaunted as he stood rocking back and forth on his snowshoes.

Lisa had welcomed Herb with a warm smile and then looked at Cindy and shrugged. "If the manager's son says that you're underage, I can't let you in the course. It's against the rules. It'll cost me my job." Lisa explained, then proceeded to lead the other six skiers past Cindy onto the lift.

"I can't believe this!" Cindy threw her gloves down in the snow and turned on Herb. "What right do you have to come up like this and interfere in a course I paid good money for? If I look eighteen I'm as good as being eighteen. I certainly can ski as well as someone eighteen!" Cindy fumed.

"You can get your money back, you know. Right over there." Herb said pointing to the Ski School registration desk. "I'll come with you so there's no snag," he offered helpfully.

"Don't bother!" Cindy growled and stormed over to the counter. She couldn't stand it any more. This whole vacation was turning into one very bad experience. First her father got hurt and put the brakes on her own skiing activities. Then she got stuck with Mollie, who could care less about learning how to ski. Now the one chance she had to really learn something about the sport was ruined. All because she was "just a kid." That is, under eighteen. Well, Cindy swore inwardly, she'd show them. She wasn't exactly sure who "them" was but it didn't matter. She had signed up for one of the races tonight during the winter carnival. It was for intermediate skiers, but tomorrow night, during the grand finale and after the beauty pageant there was going to be a moonlight race on the expert slalom course. And even if if meant being grounded for a month, Cindy Lewis was going to enter that race and win!